I0591598

I KNEW THIS WOULD HAPPEN

By

John L. Bowman

I Knew this Would Happen

Copyright 2020 John L. Bowman. All rights reserved.
Printed in the United States of America.
No part of this book may reproduced, stored in a retrieval
system, or transmitted by any means without the written
permission of the author.

ISBN 978-0-578-69872-4

Any people depicted in stock imagery are models,
which are being used for illustrative purposes only.
Because of the dynamic nature of the Internet, any web addresses
or links contained in this book may have changed
since publication and may no longer be valid.
The views expressed in this work are solely those of the author.
This book was printed on acid-free paper.

CONTENTS

CHAPTER 1

The Strange Beginning

0-20
(1950-1970)

I don't know if anyone is reading this but if you are, I must say it was so real, fascinating and painful to watch. The first time I did it alone I saw Mom and Dad and was flooded with sentiment. I had not seen my parents in over two hundred and sixty years but suddenly there they were. They looked so young and full of life—they looked too young to have children. I remembered things I had long forgotten.

The next time, I saw my childhood friends Jamie and Jay when we were about six hanging in a cherry tree eating cherries. I felt shame I had not felt in a long time for stealing Jamie's toys and I vividly recalled trying to plug a hornet nest with Jay and getting stung. I had forgotten these things.

I fast-forwarded to see my young wife Ella. I had forgotten I met her in a notorious pick-up bar in Portland. I watched myself as a hormonally driven young out on the town when I first met this beautiful brown-eyed beauty. I could not believe what a fool I was— drunken and wild. I watched as we danced and had fun and how she fortuitously gave me her telephone number. I realized how lucky I had been.

I fast-forwarded the program again and saw my now long-dead wife Ella and very young children joyously playing together. My heart was tugged seeing beautiful John and daughter Ella so young and beautiful, but I winced knowing how their lives would unfold.

I am writing this autobiography in the year 2250 AD in Old English in the Northwest Territories of Canada, which is the only place to left to live on earth because it is 70 degrees latitude north, but it is getting warmer. I feel old, my body aches, my brain doesn't work well and my heart is encrusted.

To explain all this there are two things you should know about my life—things I did not know would happen. The first is that I was the first generation of designer babies. Scientists discovered how to alter chromosomes and create designed humans which allowed parents to choose the characteristics of their offspring. Mom and Dad designed me. Mom wanted a beautiful and charming female and Dad wanted an athletic and business-minded male. Both got some of what they wanted but the doctors accidently altered my aging genome.

It was quite strange. Because of my mutated genome my aging slowed down at different rates over time. I started off at the same age as everyone else but as time passed others got older and I did not. When I was one year old everyone else was about my age but at 10 everyone was 11 and at 20 everyone was about 25. This was unnoticeable, but after 20 I began aging even slower. When I was about 30 everyone else was about 70 and at 40 everyone was 100 years old. If they lived that long. It is now 2250, I am 300 years old and all my contemporaries died long ago.

The second thing you should know is OMNI. The technological revolution that changed humankind started in the late 1900s when I was in my twenties and relentlessly advanced upon civilization. First there were computers and programs, then the internet which enabled devices like personal computers, smart phones and a plethora of internet programs and later artificial intelligence, computers that were human, a suit that makes you invisible, regenerative medicine and mental telepathy. It was an explosion never seen before.

In 2200 when I was 250 years old, the revolution culminated in a computer program named OMNI which is short for omniscient or all-knowing. The program could map the size, weight, velocity and direction of every atom which allowed it to literally map all past existence. It could not play a film of the future due to physics' Heisenberg Principle which prevented mapping atoms' future behavior. So, in short, you could watch the past but not alter it and not see the future.

I remember the first time I saw it. I walked into a small room that was a hologram of virtual reality. When commands were given through the keyboard, it reversed the atoms so I could see the past—it was like watching a movie. In a way, humankind had discovered how to travel in time. So, later in my life I visited the past often. There was a lot to see because I lived a long time.

My life was a long string of unexpected events. I have lived through civil and nuclear wars, watched an asexual human revolution, experienced the death of much of the earth, traveled to the past, lived through a killer earthquake, made and lost a fortune, became famous as an actor, politician, author and philosopher, pursued the seven deadly sins with a vengeance and have been almost killed more times than I can count. It has been one hell of a ride.

My name is Reggie Calhoun and I was born on September 25, 1950 into a traditional family that failed in Portland, Oregon which was a state in the country America that failed 190 years ago. My parents divorced when I was young, leaving us in poverty. Because I was the last of four most of my siblings had left and Mom was tired of raising children so I lived an incredibly free childhood alone with her. Mom was a lively Auntie Mamie, loved people, her children, a party and life. She always told me the worst thing in life is to be boring. Between my mother and freedom I later developed a rather adventurous, swashbuckling, self-directed and independent personality.

It has been a long time since my youth but I can remember three life-changing events from my senior year in high school like they were yesterday. The first was because I was small I was bullied—I took a lot of hits and humiliation. The second was because I was gangly the girls were not interested—I was a kind of invisible background to the opposite sex. This abruptly changed when I went to work on a ranch in eastern Oregon the summer between my junior and senior years. I spent three hard months bucking hay, eating and sleeping. When I got home Mom was startled and said what happened to you! I had grown, filled out and muscled. Back at high school the bullying problem came to an abrupt end when I picked up Bob Peterson, my main tormentor, by the neck and threatened to beat him to a pulp. The second change surprised me—girls started smiling and flirting with me.

I love women and there have been many in my life as you will discover, but my relationship with the first ones did not go well. The most beautiful girl in school was red-haired fair-skinned Betsy, whom I had always admired from a distance. To my surprise she started talking to me, our friendship flourished and we fell in love. My first sex was in the cramped back seat of my mom's car with her—it was not so much sex but rather a contortion act. We became a couple. Around the middle of my last year out of nowhere Betsy said she had accepted a date from another guy. I was dumbfounded and for a short time insanely jealous. I asked her why and she said she just wanted to know other boys. I said if you do this we are done and she laughed and said it was no big deal. She dated the boy and our love affair abruptly died.

Out of curiosity I returned to Betsy's life a few times through OMNI. It turns out she was quite loose and disloyal. She went to college for about a year, married a man who looked like her father, had two children, they both cheated on each other and they divorced. The last time I visited her she was working in a restaurant, poor and very unhappy. Her beauty had faded like her fortune. I learned from Betsy that character and life decisions have a lot to do with how life turns out—a lesson that was driven home by other women later.

The third event occurred because I had been a lazy, dull screw-off in school academically, earning mediocre grades. One day early in my senior year out of nowhere anxiously it occurred to me high school was almost over and what was I to do next! I wondered what would become of me and for the first time in life began pondering my future.

I decided I needed to go to college so I buckled down, took my academics seriously and started rigorously taking notes in class, studying, reading and getting up early in the morning to prepare for exams. To my teachers' and other students' amazement my C's suddenly became straight A's, I made the Dean's List and was selected valedictorian. I applied to some colleges, including one longshot, Oxford, which to my amazement accepted me. Mr. Hansen, my school counselor, who had long ago relegated me to an appliance repairman, was utterly mystified.

So, in 1969 at age 18 I flew to Oxford, England and started a life in high academia. It was a different, fascinating and hard strange new world. Unlike America, English society had stratified classes like commoners and royalty. The city of Oxford was small, intimate and livable—the perfect university town. Historic Oxford itself had not changed since the Middle Ages with its Gothic spires, Baroque porticoes and Georgian courtyards and intense academic atmosphere. As a fresher I got a '60s flat at Trinity College with Charlie Marlboro who I had met at a pub. I started going to classes and attending social events like white-tie balls and guest night formal dinners. I often went to the King's Arms pub in the evening to drink bitter with Charlie. As time passed I acclimated and began using their words like sconce (requiring a person drink a tankard of ale for breaching etiquette) and rustificate (to temporarily leave the university). My intense academic life involved lectures, papers, tutors, tests and finals. I would often do all-nighters studying and spend hours taking exams over days. I majored in two areas that particularly interested me—philosophy and finance.

My second relationship with a woman was at Oxford and went no better than my first. Charlie and I became close friends and he kept telling me that I had to meet his sister Madeline because we looked so much alike. One day I agreed and met her at a party at their house. I was in a greeting line when our eyes met. She was utterly captivating. I said I don't know whether to introduce myself, kiss you, make love to you or marry you and she laughed and said why don't we just introduce ourselves first. We walked in the garden, kissed and our love affair bloomed for a couple of years. She was the prettiest girl in the county, hotly pursued and sexy but sometimes strangely cold and reserved. I fell deeply in love with Madeline so near the end of my senior year I asked her to marry me. With tears in her eyes she said no because her mother thought I was not socially prominent. She said she loved me but her station made it impossible. I said goodbye and thought being unlucky in love may be my lot in life. I never went back in time to visit her because it would be too painful.

Betsy's lack of loyalty and Madeline's mother's snobbery taught me a few lessons about love, rejection and heart pain. But I had received a good education at Oxford and had been transformed into an intellectual interested in life and learning. I also learned a new aspect of my character, which was the love of adventure. So, the day I graduated from Oxford I decided to take some time off and go look around. Rather than go home to Portland, I hitchhiked to the port of Southampton looking for something new in life.

CHAPTER 2

The Road not Taken

20-22
(1970-1990)

I went back and looked at myself hitchhiking to Southampton in 1973 a few times and was thrilled to see my excitement so typical of youth. During my ride I was trying to remember Robert Frost's poem *The Road Not Taken* but all I could recall was *two roads diverging in a yellow wood and I took the one less traveled.* The poem spoke to me because I had decided to take the less-traveled road rather than pursue conventional goals like career and family like my classmates. I remembered at that time in my life I was driven by the thought that I have only one life to live so I must make the most of it. It was energizing to watch me so young, full of passion for adventure, supremely happy and alive. I was grateful to be healthy, educated and, having inherited a small amount of money, it was a great time of my life. Little did I know then what I was getting in for.

The port at Southampton was chaotic. Ships were coming, unloading and loading and going, it was crowded and the noise was deafening. I had a vague idea of catching a ride on some ship to an exotic destination but destiny sent me in another direction. I went to a bar to have a beer to ponder my next move, unknowing it was full of procurers—agents who shanghai people to work on tramp steamers for a fee. My beer was drugged, I passed out and when I woke up I was in a dirty bunk in a small, dark and odious cabin. I was roused, manhandled and immediately put to work at the dirtiest jobs like cleaning latrines, washing dishes and mopping dirty floors. My life-adventure was not starting well. In the evening when I was free on deck at sea I began to think otherwise—I was glad to have forgotten Madeline, her mother and past disappointments. Schweitzer was right. Happiness truly is good health and a poor memory.

It turned out I was on a cargo ship taking war material to Vietnam. It took an interminable two months to round Cape Horn and arrive at Hawaii to refuel. It was a slow freighter. To escape my fate I jumped ship, hitchhiked to Honolulu, went into a bar, ran into the first mate and crewmembers who tackled me and hauled me back to the boat. We finally docked at Saigon after having spent another month doing all the shit jobs on the boat.

The Vietnam War between the Americans and Communist North Vietnam had started in 1964 and after nine years of fighting and the loss of over 50,000 American lives, it was still intense. When we docked there was gunfire and heavy shelling in the distance. The captain was anxious to leave as soon as possible so the ship was quickly unloaded and immediately set out to sea. I was so relieved to be escaping I joined a few crewmen drinking an awful distilled whiskey, got roaring drunk, stumbled over some rigging, hit the rail and fell overboard. Inebriated I swam to shore and fell asleep.

I woke in the morning to a deafening gun battle over the crest of the hill. I crawled to the top and saw a squad of American troops in front of me in a fearful firefight against a throng of advancing ragged Viet Cong. An American sergeant saw me and yelled to man the fifty-caliber machine gun. Unthinking I crawled to the gun, pushed the dead gunner away, found the trigger and started firing. It was exhilarating as I methodically flattened throngs of the advancing troops, felt bullets within inches of my head. Being in mortal danger was better than cleaning toilets. The enemy retreated. We stood and roared with victory cheers, holding our guns high while an army reporter took our picture. I later learned that we had been instrumental in helping stop the Tet Offensive along the coast but during the hoopla I slipped away and quickly headed east.

My only thought was to escape the war zone as I headed toward Kampuchea and Laos unknowing that the war had been expanded to these regions in the 1970s. I walked most of the 200 miles to Phnum Pénh occasionally getting rides, once on an ox cart, and sometimes taking a bus. I traveled as fast as I could always avoiding pervasive violence. In spite of their ferocious reputation I found most Vietnamese good and hospitable and proud of their culture. It seemed to me that the invasion of cold, brutal and lifeless communism was sapping these good people of their vitality. It is a political philosophy that makes ideology more important than people, evident by the largely listless and empty villages I went through.

One village in western Kampuchea horrified me. I had heard that the communists were conducting purification and re-programming programs and what I found was ethnic cleansing, pogroms and death. The communists were in the process of cleansing this village. As I entered I heard wailing and gunfire in the distance where villagers were being killed. I avoided everyone as I rapidly slid out of town until I came to a hut with muted crying and sobbing inside. I looked in the door and saw maybe 25 children and a couple of adults huddled in terror. To this day I do not know why but I instinctively gestured to follow me. It was one of those brief magical moments in life when these children looked into my eyes with hope—I can only think they saw a big, white, red-haired Scotsman that did not look like the short brown men killing their parents—they thought I was a god. They followed me in a quiet line like ducklings follow their mother and we snaked out of town into the safety of the jungle. After a few miles we stopped, one old man took a photo of me with the children and I told the adults to take them further into the wild to hide. I was shaking with fear and anxiety as they moved off when another villager offered to give me a ride on his small 125 cc Honda motorcycle 200 miles to Bangkok. I gladly accepted but later regretted it because my butt hurt due to the small seat and bumpy ride.

He dropped me off in the red-light district of Bangkok. After many months traveling the dark unpopulated countryside I was overwhelmed by the crowds and bright artificial neon lights. I thanked him and went into the nearest bar, the Rose, for a beer, but it turned out to be a brothel. I felt exhausted and lonely when the madam summoned five mostly naked young Thai girls to stand in front of me and asked who I wanted. I looked at them, felt pity, tremendous sorrow for their fate and I declined the offer. The pleasant looking small one on the end caught my eye and I asked if I could just talk with her. The skeptical madam was surprised and said, "five dollars." So, I spent the next three hours in engaging conversation with Noy.

Noy was a beautiful young Thai woman with passable English, bountiful intelligence and, like many Asian women, deferential to men and eager to please. Talking with Noy was like telling all your deepest thoughts to an understanding stranger knowing you will never see them again—a rare human relationship. Noy and I got to know each other intimately and in time at her apartment made love constantly. For her sex was like going to the bathroom. It was entirely natural. It made me think of the stilted and unnatural western sexual norms and Hester in Nathanael Hawthorne's *Scarlet Letter* who was made to wear a scarlet "A" signifying an adulterer.

I fell in love with my little Noy but after a few weeks, one night while waiting in the Rose for Noy to get off of work, someone slipped a drug into my beer. I went into terrifying and nightmarish madness, slipping in and out of consciousness. I had a recurring dream where I was standing on the edge of a cliff with my beautiful girlfriend and she pushed me off. As I was falling I would always wonder why she did it and the dream would end just before I hit the rocks. When I awoke two months later in Noy's apartment I was dirty, smelly, disheveled, dehydrated and emaciated. My first thought was that Timothy Leary, the LSD advocate who always wanted to get to the other side, was right. There is another side and it is called hell.

Noy was mysteriously gone. For the next two weeks I slept, ate and drank vociferously and gradually regained my health and sanity. With OMNI looking back in the future I learned later that it was Noy who had slipped me the LSD because she loved me and could not bear saying goodbye. I also learned that Noy could be fierce when she needed to be. She had joined the resistance against communism and was killed in an ambush in northern Laos.

I traveled north by bus through Thailand, Burma and then India until I hit the southern flank of the majestic Himalayas and then westerly to Siliguri, India where there was a road that went north through a gap in the mountains. It was an unreal winding road that snaked its treacherous way through deep valleys and high cold and snowy passes that ended in mystical Lhasa, Tibet, the crucible of Buddhism and home of the Dali Lama. Unfortunately he had fled because the communist Chinese had invaded the country, subjugated the population and were trying to eliminate religion. Because of Lhasa's altitude, I immediately got altitude sickness, felt like puking, checked into a hostel and stayed in bed for two days.

The third day I got up early in the cool and clear morning and walked downtown and around the Portola Palace amongst the smell of incense, prayer mantras and Tibetans spinning their golden prayer wheels. Lhasa was a magical mystical place, but the mood of the people was gloomy, silent and resentful at the Chinese military's presence. I passed an anti-Chinese demonstration as I hiked to the top of the Palace entrance where I was confronted by a plainclothes Chinese officer who quickly slipped away when he learned I was an American.

Inside the Palace was like a medieval monastery—dark, dirty and damp with many red-robed Buddhist priests chanting and bowing before holy butter lamps. I struck up a conversation with one weary priest who could speak English and learned that they were in great danger because the Chinese were in the process of liquidating them. Reflex-like, I said let's get out of here now and like the children in Kampuchea about ten of them obediently followed me. I had no idea how to get them out but instinctively purloined the Palace bus and drove to the airport. It was heavily guarded so I drove around to the back, crashed through a maintenance gate and raced to a group of parked airplanes. The priests quickly got on the plane grateful but disgusted because I was throwing up from fear and the remnants of altitude sickness.

I had never flown a plane but Fortune was with me because this piston-prop older Beechcraft Bonanza was perfect. When I was young I played the very old virtual video game *Fly Now!* and had practiced on this very plane. I settled into the pilot seat, surveyed the familiar instrument panel, found the throttle, brakes and flaps, started the engines, taxied to the runway, revved the engines and took off. Luckily it had a full tank of gas so I knew with a range of about 880 miles it just might make New Delhi so I climbed to 10,000 ft. and headed southwest. It was both exhilarating and eerie to be flying for the first time at night amongst chanting Buddhist monks. After a few hours I saw city lights and a runway, lowered the flaps, descended, landed and taxied to a sign that read New Delhi International Airport ARCO refilling station. As they got out one monk took a photo of us all together, I refueled the plane and took off into the night.

I decided I had enough of Asia, so I headed west toward the Middle East and Europe. Initially I was lucky because unopposed I was able to refuel at Karachi, Pakistan, Oman on the Arabian Peninsula and Baghdad. My luck ran out over eastern Turkey when I ran out of gas and crashed landed in a field near Ephesus. The plane was wrecked but I survived and wandered in the dark until I found what I thought was an empty farmhouse where I fell asleep. I woke up in the library at Ephesus surrounded by a bunch of curious tourists wearing Bermuda shorts and Hawaiian shirts. I quickly stumbled out, made my way to the nearest port and caught a ferry west to Greece.

It felt good to be back in familiar western civilization. Looking back this was, as Dickens wrote, the best and worst of times in my three-hundred-year life. The ferry's first stop was the remote Aegean Island of Ios so I decided to get off and look around. I climbed through the all-white Greek village to the crest of the hill and saw enchanting Mylopotas bay, with its deep blue water and white crescent-shaped sandy beach, I was breathless. To my delight on the beach there were hundreds of mostly naked young people from many countries playing, dancing and swimming. I wandered into the local hangout Far Out, ordered a beer and pondered my future. Deep in thought a soft voice asked me my name so I turned and saw this absolutely gorgeous smiling red-haired twentyish fair-skinned Irish beauty. I was struck, we stared at each other for a while, I managed to say Reggie, she said she was Tricia and then we talked, drank and laughed until the sun rose over the bay in the morning. This was the beginning of my best times.

I often go back in time to see this woman I fell in love with. She had just finished school at Trinity College in Dublin and was taking time to travel. She was soft, warm, friendly, easygoing, fun, joyful and above all sensuous—she loved skin. Her only foibles were an Irish temper and a phobia about people putting their fingers in their belly button. But, like me, she was anxious to enjoy her short time of existence. We became a couple and spent the early part of the 1980s wandering together around Europe with a backpack, mostly by train and staying in hostels. Together we visited historic sites, studied European history, met a variety of interesting people in different cultures, drank and danced and made love. We walked the romantic Seine together in Paris, drank beer in the rowdy Hofbrauhaus in Munich, partied late at cabarets in Paris and sang the songs of the 1965 film classic *Sound of Music* in Saltsburg.

During this time, I often reflected on Europe's contradictions. On the surface it was rich in history and culture but under the surface I often saw darkness. When I first visited the spectacular ruins of the Coliseum I was awed but struck by the thought that so many had lost their lives in it. At the obelisk of Luxor in the beautiful Palace de la Concorde garden in Paris I recalled that it marked the spot where 40,000 people had been guillotined during the French Revolution Reign of Terror, and in Prague, Jews had been rounded up by Nazis and sent to their death in concentration camps. It occurred to me that civilization has a dark side. Unbeknownst to me I was about to witness that darkness firsthand in the worst of times.

The 1980s were a period of horrible terrorist bomb attacks in Europe. From Greece Tricia and I traveled to Bologna, Italy, were we were sitting in a sidewalk cafe when the Revoluzionari detonated a bomb fifty feet from us, killing 85 people. The percussion knocked me to the ground, I blacked out for a minute, woke up dazed and deaf surrounded by broken windows, debris, blood and body parts. It was horrifying to see ripped arms, feet, torsos and heads on the ground that only a minute ago had been part of a person. Later we read about other terrorist bombings like suicidal Gundolf Köhler who self-exploded at an Oktoberfest in West Germany killing 13 people, when the Irish Republican Army exploded a bomb in London's Hyde Park killing 11 people in 1982 and later that year bombed Droppin Well killing 17 people. I had been in many death scrapes during my adventures but had never seen anything like this. It was awful to have experience the deaths of some of the over 500 killed or seriously maimed people over the short period of two years. But the worst was yet to come.

To escape the mayhem Tricia and I took a ferry to Dublin, Ireland. We went to Galway to visit her parents who were welcoming but distant. They preferred she marry an Irish man. She was happy to be home and enrolled in an airline stewardess training program with Ireland's Aer Lingus, which had been one of her lifelong dreams. We were in love and excitedly talked about marrying and starting a family together despite her parents but our dreams were delayed when the mayhem resumed. The IRA had been at war with the British since the 1972 Bloody Sunday that instigated British rule of Northern Ireland. Tricia and I were sitting in the bar of the Brighton Grand Hotel drinking wine in 1984 where many British politicians, including Prime Minister Margret Thatcher, were negotiating a peace agreement when I noticed two wary looking young Irish men in long coats enter. I immediately recognized terrorist bombers—Grim Reapers with their satchel-scythes who bring death. I jumped, ran to the security detail and screamed BOMBERS then turned and tackled the first bomber. We struggled and with the help of others subdued the man but the other blew himself up with a 100-pound bomb killing six soldiers and a few politicians along with thirty-four people who were injured. I spent two weeks in the hospital recovering from my wounds.

When I was released from the hospital Tricia and I decided we had enough of terrorist violence so on a lark we packed our clothes and flew on one of her stewardess flights to Lima, Peru. We figured we could escape the carnage on the other side of the globe. The flight was smooth until over the Andes the plane lost one of its hydraulic systems and began wildly gyrating. The pilots struggled to land at

Lima International Airport, but it flipped and cartwheeled down the runway. It felt like going over Niagara Falls in a barrel. Along with some other lucky passengers I was thrown from the plane which caught fire and incinerated. Eleven passengers were killed, including Tricia. I was numb with grief watching the firefighters remove her lifeless charred body from the wreckage. It was a strange time of my life. I was in an alien land, injured and again having lost another love of my life. I was devastated and it took weeks to recover my strength and sanity. Through OMNI I often go back in time to see Tricia and see her beautiful, loving and radiant face but it always made me sad knowing that a life with her was not to be. All I could do was to keep living so I moved on.

The death of Tricia made me tired and want to go home, but my lack of money compelled me on. The armored vehicles surrounding Lima's presidential palace did not portend well so I headed north. In 1941 there had been a border war between Peru and Ecuador. Peru had invaded and occupied the Cordillera del Cóndor southern portion of Ecuador. There had been numerous skirmishes over of the years in this region and much carnage. I was traversing this area in a bus when some Ecuadorian soldiers stopped it, took some Peruvian men off the bus and shot them in plain sight. The women and children were screaming and crying when my adrenaline kicked in. I tackled the driver, struggled and pushed him out the door, grabbed the wheel and gunned it out of there under a hail of bullets. We drove north on dirt roads until we came to what looked like a peaceful village, they got out and I drove on north until the road ended in Buenaventura on the Colombian coast. I quickly ditched the bus in the crowed city and hired on to a fishing boat that was going to the coastal city Managua in Nicaragua.

On landing in Nicaragua, I hoped the violence was over only to find myself immersed in a civil war between the Soviet Union backed leftist Sandinistas and American-backed Contras. The Contras were rebel groups that opposed the communist Nicaraguan government that had been overtly lauded and secretly supported by then-American president Ronald Reagan. It was the late 1980s and the bloody war had become a proxy war of the Cold War, thus gaining international attention.

In a crowded Central American city like Managua, a tall, white and red-haired American stood out like a sore thumb amongst throngs of short, dark-skinned people so it was only natural when I saw Lee Abbott, another tall white American, we were drawn together. Lee had fought in Vietnam, then gone home to his wife and two children in the States, but was incapable of adjusting to civilian life due to post-traumatic stress disorder. He had come to Nicaragua as a mercenary solider to escape civilization and its benumbing effects. He was a cheerful and affable character and together we worked our way north avoiding bandits and soldiers. Near Motagalpa we ran into a unit of Contra fighters who, seeing that we were Americans, tried to recruit us. Lee was eager but I was wary because I had heard some bad things about these guerillas. They took us on an ugly sortie to one Sandinista village where they raped, tortured, mutilated and killed civilians. I was horrified and slipped away in the night and again headed north. With OMNI, I went back once to find out what happened to Lee. He had joined the Contras and was killed in a deadly firefight later that year in a secret American airbase in northern Costa Rica.

It was the late 1980s when I made it to the Mexican border. I was close to home, but I still had to traverse the cartel drug wars that were raging at that time. Most Americans see the safe coastal tourist cities like Cancun and Puerto Vallarta but it was different in the interior. The Gulf Cartel's private mercenary army Los Zetas was in a turf war with the Tijuana Cartel led by murderous drug lord Pablo Gaviria who was called the world's greatest outlaw. It was dangerous to travel anywhere in the interior due to random daily shootings, gun battles and mass executions. I saw pervasive fear, terrified citizens and many empty dead villages. I had to be invisible because I could get shot at any time from anywhere, so I avoided main roads and cities. It was a patchwork of deadly cartel traps and traversing it was like walking through a minefield.

The closest I came to death during my travels was in the small Gulf Cartel village of Saín Alto in a small local grocery store trying to be inconspicuous when a gang of Tijuana Cartel members entered with automatic machine guns and began spraying it with their guns. Bullets skimmed my head. People were getting killed left and right and blood was everywhere. My adrenaline kicked in, I sprinted to a window, dove through it and ran as fast as I could for miles. I was lucky to have lived.

I eventually made it to the border, elatedly crossed into America and hitchhiked up I-5 to Portland. It felt good to be back in the clean, clear and peaceful Northwest.

This period of my life taught me something about humans—they are a violent lot. Everywhere I went in the world there had been conflict, violence and death. Man is indeed a wolf to man and Freud was right when he wrote in *Civilization and its Discontents* that humans are naturally violent because civilization suppresses their aggressive instinct. But it had been a grand adventure. It had been a spontaneous, exciting and thrilling experience. Looking back, I was glad that I had taken the less-traveled adventurous road. But I was now ready for something new in life.

CHAPTER 3

The Biologic Urge

23-27
(1990-2040)

My impression of the clean and peaceful Northwest was shattered when I got to Portland. I saw streets full of ragged, wild mentally disturbed people, tents and homelessness, garbage, human waste, drugs, sometimes violent street protests and ubiquitous strip clubs. It looked like a society that had lost its moral compass and anything goes. I was reminded of the assassin's creed from my philosophy classes where when nothing is true everything is permitted. Portland had changed.

I was also stunned to see my old Portland friends who were in their late thirties and married with children. I had been gone 20 years but only aged two—I looked about 22 years old and they all noticed. I learned that my father had died and Mom, who was in her late sixties and very sick, was living alone. I visited her for one of the last times. It was an emotional experience seeing her again, talking about the past and watching her cry over my not having a father. I had a chance to tell her that it had been very painful but ironically had caused an inner strength that had propelled me to successes in life. We smiled, we told each other we loved each other, we laughed and we hugged—

it felt great. She died a few weeks later from cancer. I was at her bedside when she died, I watched trancelike as they took her body away, stared at her empty bed for a long time and then saw the red watch she had worn only hours earlier, now alone without an owner, and felt a deep sense of grief. When my mother—my crucible—died, part of me did also.

Up to now my life had been mostly schooling and travel but there was always something missing. I had enough of both and was now feeling an irresistible urge for something more enduring in life. I now know what I wanted was meaning and I found it in the timeless biologic instinct to reproduce. I decided I wanted to marry, have children and live a normal life. But I needed a woman so I set out to find one. It was odd because men usually do not plan to find a woman to love and reproduce with. Rather they just occur. Love cannot be manufactured. Also, I was a little nervous because my first encounters with the opposite sex had not gone well. But I needed a good woman and decided to find one.

I thought about finding one at a church social but I was an atheist, or among my friends but they were too old. I also had to deal with my feelings about the women in my past that I had lost: Betsy, Madeline, Noy and Tricia. These had been painful experiences. But I still wanted a woman so I decided to go the notorious gaudy pick-up bar the Turquoise Room.

My expectations were low when I walked into the dark, crowded smoke-filled joint, sat at a table alone and ordered a beer. Next to me was a table of five or six young women drinking and laughing so I glanced at them and saw Ella. Even today I remember how utterly captivated I was when I first saw her. She was a brown-haired beauty with a huge enchanting smile and sparkling brown eyes that looked just like my mother's. My theory is that I had spent babyhood in a crib looking at mother's big brown loving eyes and now those same eyes were looking back at me across a dark smoke-filled bar. I was captured.

Ella was from a small town near Portland, Estacada. She had just turned 21 and her girlfriends were taking her out to big town Portland to celebrate. I asked her to dance, we talked, flirted and she gave me her telephone number. Expectantly I called her the next day for a date and she turned me down. I called her two more times and disappointingly she again turned me down. I thought to myself that getting a woman is not easy. Undeterred I called her a fourth time and she reluctantly agreed to meet me at the Dublin Pub for a drink. Her first words were that I had red hair. We quietly talked, exchanged life stories, laughed and enjoyed each other's easy company. Thus began our romance; we went on picnics, walks and to the beach where one time I taught her how to drive a clutch and quietly grimaced as she ground through my car's gears. We made love for the first time at the beach and the love affair of my life began.

It turned out I was not to be unlucky in love. Ella was a really good woman, she was beautiful, cheerful, moral, loyal and frugal. She had an infectious smile that would light up a room and the people around her. She had an irresistible sense of humor and loved to laugh. She once asked a woman at the grocery store with a cart full of bananas if she lived with monkeys. Once after blowing out her birthday candles she asked if she was thinner. Another time, after I accidently ruined her battery-powered coffee frother she mischievously asked me not to run the toaster through the dishwasher again. She was also Rubenesque, buxom and sensuous. She loved her family and friends and shared experiences so when I asked her parents for permission to marry her we hatched a plan for her upcoming birthday party. Her mother invited our friends and family, I got on a knee and proposed to her, she laughed, cried and said yes to everyone's excitement and joy. We had a big church wedding and started procreating children.

I choke with emotion, sentimentality and longing when I recall this fairytale period of my life. I spent the next fifty years with Ella raising John, Sybil, Maude, Pete, Ella and Edward. It was a time of family and friends. We joined many clubs in Portland and had a gay social life. I used my degree in finance from Oxford to start a financial services company, Reggie Calhoun Securities and Investment Advisors Inc., that succeeded beyond my wildest dreams. I started it in Portland but it grew into a national chain within twenty years and made us rich. With our newfound wealth Ella and I took the family on many international trips and bought a 10,000 sq. ft. mansion with a pool, tennis court and library to live in. It was the happiest and most meaningful period of my life.

I lived through many catastrophes in my life but one of the worst was the Richter scale 9.2 great Northwest Earthquake in 2021. It occurs every 300 to 600 years and because it was overdue scientists had been predicting it for some time. The Cascadia Subduction Zone, 100 miles of the West Coast where the Juan de Fuca Plate is sliding beneath the North American Plate, moved creating a destructive force equal to a nuclear blast or an asteroid strike. It was one of the worst natural disasters in American history. The quake convulsed the West Coast for five minutes. Bridges failed, soil liquefied, brick and masonry buildings shattered, some skyscrapers in Portland and Seattle toppled and city centers like Portland and Seattle were buried in glass shards and rubble. It created a 50 ft. tsunami that ripped coastal regions clean off the map, pulverized everything and killed everyone in its path.

Ella and I were in the house on a quiet Sunday alone (our children were grown and gone by this time) when it suddenly struck around 10 in the morning. The house shook violently for what seemed an interminable time, windows blasted out and debris flew everywhere. We had worked out in advance an escape plan to our family property at Mt. Hood fifty miles outside Portland. The property was a four-acre remote campsite on the wild Salmon River. It had been in my family for 100 years and I had gone there all my life camping and picnicking. We called it Arrah Wanna. Our first moves were to load my Honda 750 Shadow motorcycle with provisions including a siphon, grab my 38-caliber handgun and head east.

With Ella on the back I maneuvered around fallen trees and telephone poles, sparking electrical wires, crevasses in the road, downed overpasses, abandoned cars and injured or dead people. To go east we had to cross the Willamette River, but all of the bridges had collapsed except the newest one designed for such an earthquake: Tillicum Bridge. Incredibly we got to it and crossed to the entrance to the Springwater Corridor bicycle route to the small city of Boring about 20 miles outside Portland. As we raced east through the chaos and destruction we were accosted by many desperate roaming people seeking food, water or medical help. At one point a gang of threatening youths blocked our route and tried to pull us off the bike. We only escaped when I fired a shot in the air and raced off. Occasionally siphoning gas from abandoned cars we made good time riding the shoulder of Highway 26 east to avoid the huge traffic jam of people trying to escape until we found the last bridge over the Salmon River collapsed. We backtracked and took an alternate route up old Barlow Trail Road and made it to Arrah Wanna. Hundreds of thousands of people died in the earthquake but all of my children and some other relatives survived. We lived a rugged pioneer life for months there as Northwest civilization gradually returned to normal and eventually went back to Portland and began rebuilding our lives. It was a harrowing experience and one really exciting bike ride.

As I mentioned earlier my repressed aging process was due to early bioengineering. Doctors had accidently modified my genome for aging so I aged slower than others as time progressed. As bioengineering advanced it created a plethora of problems. The first was who is to live. It had eliminated most causes of death; a gene-altering nasal spray would cure cancer and a computer program could rebuild a damaged heart. So, the world became overpopulated and human needs exceeded earth's ability to provide. Inevitably, the loathsome question of who would die so others could live emerged. The second was who was to be born. Biology demonstrated that some human traits increase survivability so a eugenics debate over what kind of humans should exist took place. The third problem was the loss of identity. Bioengineering could change our chromosomes and who we are—including our personality. A hormonally driven fifteen-year-old girl could suddenly become a sixty-year-old experienced man and vice versa. Who we are as humans became a blur and many traditions like marriage, differences like gender and sexual orientation became obsolete. The problem was that humans were unprepared to be god and could only stupidly blunder their way through this bioengineering morass of new issues.

I was about 30 when the bombshell *New York Times* article appeared and my past caught up with me. I was in the office when my secretary raced in waving an article titled "The Unknown Warrior," excitedly asking if this was me. I could not believe what I read. It described an unknown warrior with a collage of photos of me with a machine gun in Vietnam, saving child from guerillas in Thailand, deplaning rescued monks in New Delhi, struggling with a bomb terrorist in Ireland and driving a bus saving people in Peru. I was also purported to have fought with the Contras in Nicaragua and against the drug cartels in Mexico. Overnight I became a celebrity. I had a lot of explaining to do to amazed Ella, my children, family members, friends and co-workers.

But with fame, my anonymity gone and increasing interest in me things started to get strange. Some of the photos of me were taken over fifty years ago when I looked in my early twenties and now I was only 30. People began to wonder and ask questions why I looked so young and the story of my slow aging spread like wildfire-I became an uncomfortable curiosity. To make matters worse Ella, my children, my friends and everyone I knew were getting older than me. I was only 30 and many were in their sixties and seventies and sick.

The strangest of all was what happened to my children. Ella and I had six children together: John, Sybil, Maude, Pete, Ella and Edward. I watched each of their lives unfold because I outlived them all. John was handsome, full of vinegar, serious and earnest but also clumsy, quick to anger, error prone and often morose. He worked like a dog in his business, ignored his family, divorced, his business failed, he became an alcoholic and tragically died from a heart attack at age 41. Sybil was a red-haired beauty who was a warm, funny, adventurous-glad–to-be-alive woman who was comfortable in her skin. She never married, had no children and disappeared while hiking from Mexico to Canada alone on the Pacific Crest Trail, never to be found. Maude and Ella were cut from the same cloth. They both were beauties like their mother, they married, had many children and lived conventional happy and meaningful lives. Pete hated the Northwest rain, moved to Florida and we lost touch with him. Our youngest, Edward, inherited the family business mind, went to Harvard Business School and became president of General Motors.

At first my children teased me about the family's longevity genes but this changed to curiosity and resentment when they started getting older than me. One of the hardest things for me was to watch my children get old and sick. But the worst came in 2030 when sixty-year-old Ella got cancer. Numb, I watched her get sick, grieve when the doctor told her she had terminal cancer, gradually become weak, pallid, gaunt, yellow and bedridden. We talked a lot in her final days about our past, children and joys. In spite of her pain throughout her ordeal she never lost her happy cheerful spirit. Ella died at age 61 on September 20, 2031.

I was devastated. Not only had I now lost Betsy, Madeline, Noy and Tricia but also the love of my life, my partner in life, my wife, the mother of my children and my life companion-she went away forever. I was so disoriented my children had to handle the funeral while I could only attend in a comatose state. Over time my grief gradually subsided, I regained my senses, said goodbye to Ella at her grave and moved on because I was still alive. I thought about her often for the rest of my life.

The real shocker came when I was in my early thirties when my children started dying. Like most parents I expected to enjoy my children's marriages, grandchildren and then die. Some like John and Sybil had died young but the others were alive but older than me. Today I wince knowing that the cures for the diseases they died from, mostly cancer and heart disease, were only a few years away. I became the anomaly-grandfather who does not age and witnesses the passing of generations of relatives, including most of his children, who was only in his early thirties.

I often used OMNI to go back in time to visit my now-ancient family. I loved seeing my beloved Ella and young children. It was the happiest time of my life. When I was living in this era of my life the challenges I faced sometimes clouded my perspective which diminished my appreciation for what I had. I now know what a lucky man I had been.

So, I had spent fifty years of my life married, raising a family and growing a business but I was only about 32 with much more life ahead. In 2040, when my wife was gone and my children had moved on, I began feeling depressed and alone. My fairytale life was over. I was also weary of other people's growing curiosity about my age. I got tired of trying to explain something I did not understand. To escape living under a microscope and avoid attention I began moving to new places. In each new town I hid my secret and keep my true self hidden. I wore Shakespeare's mask for the rest of my life.

My first move was to a small isolated cowboy town in then-eastern Oregon called Burns.

CHAPTER 4

A Pig Satisfied

27-32
(2041-2060)

I was sitting in my office in an altered state of mind when I decided I wanted to do something different. I drove home, changed into my jogging clothes and, like Forrest Gump just started jogging east on Highway 26 to the small, ranch and cowboy central Oregon town of Burns about 300 miles away. I just dropped everything including my house, business and remaining friends and family and started running.

At first I could only do five miles a day but as I got into shape it increased to 10 and eventually 20. I would usually sleep just off the road, eat beef jerky and later in the desert learned that water could usually be found near cottonwood trees. I felt an enlivening sense of freedom jogging through the dense high cool and forested Cascades, but I got a spiritual attachment to the wide-open eastern Oregon desert. After jogging away from the last bastion of civilization, Bend, into the primal desert I felt like I was returning to nature. After all the events of my life it felt good to be isolated and alone amongst the sweet smell of sagebrush and juniper, the dry heat and warm evening breezes. At night I felt deep silence, experienced utter darkness and saw brilliant starry skies. It felt good to free, alive with no cares in the world. I felt vital and my aging process seemed to slow even more.

This all made me quite philosophic. I thought about how much human civilization judges and defines us, making us what we are not. I thought how the desolate desert makes conspicuous the artificial roles and masks of society. Running alone in the desert made me think about how meaningless the temporary structures of humankind are and how insignificant my past life cares were. Running under the white floating clouds and blue sky with a 360-degree view of desert expanse made me think about how my freedom had been suppressed in civilized Portland. Knowing that the desert view never changed whether I was there or not made me realize I was more than what others say but rather part of some grander plan.

Human's biology evolved in nature under the open skies, bright stars and hot suns, not crowded cities. Our bodies are programmed to go to sleep at dusk and wake with the dawn. The rhythms of the desert forged our natures and returning to it caused me to return to my prehistoric natural self. I realized how much human civilization had accelerated time and upset my biologic rhythms. Now I was jogging alone in the desert relaxed and at peace.

Somewhere along the line I noticed a few buzzards circulating overhead but thought nothing of it. As time progressed, however, I noticed more were circling and began to wonder if they knew something I did not. Eventually, they began dive-bombing me so I took to throwing rocks at them. It became quite a spectacle until after three weeks of jogging I entered the final grade to Burns and they all disappointedly disappeared.

I jogged straight to the first restaurant I found, the Burns Cookhouse and asked the owner for a job. He said the only opening was for a dishwasher at $1,000 a month. I asked if he knew of any cheap rooms for rent and he said the Standard Motel a few blocks away rents rooms by the month. I took the job, jogged to the ransacked motel and rented a run down, drab room with a black and white television for $450 a month. I fell on the bed, slept for 12 hours and woke up feeling great. I loved the irony of it all; a millionaire businessman with a big house in Portland washing dishes and living in a motel room in Burns, Oregon. I found it a pleasure to be completely unknown, carefree, invisible and with no life obligations.

I became a regular at the local pub, the Pine Tavern drinking beer, watching football and playing pool. My existence became mundane, I became a slob, I stopped thinking and I was obliviously happy. It was at the Pine that I met Stella who was also a regular. Stella was a tragic figure. She was a 26-year-old small-town girl who had never been outside Burns. Her continence was plain but she had an earthy and sexy way about her. She had a curvaceous body and wore revealing clothes to advertise it. Initially we just talked, laughed and went home inebriated and sometimes had sex. As time passed our conversations became deeper and more meaningful as we described our inner feelings and aspirations. Inside, Stella was a wonderful loving, caring and innocently trusting person. Outside, she had become rather hardened, sometimes sarcastic rudely venting her hurt feelings through her guttural smokers voice. I don't think Stella ever quite believed my life story, but she was intrigued with my knowledge and grateful for my attention.

Recalling Stella's life makes me sad. Because she was not particularly attractive she had been passed over by all the local boys and all of her high school girlfriends had married and were pregnant with children and raising families. She desperately wanted a husband, children and family of her own and everyone in town knew it. But fate had relegated her to the society's lowest level and she ended up giving her body freely for love but never getting it in return. Stella was the small-town slut used by all the men. It was saddening for me to see a vibrant, healthy, happy and eager young woman whose biologic aspirations were thwarted only because she was not attractive. It was hard for me to witness the pain, solitude and dejection she experienced. Around 2055 I went back in OMNI to visit Stella. I found her in her early forties still in Burns alone, depressed and destitute. She died from alcoholism shortly after my last visit and nobody had said goodbye. Strangely, Stella had ignited one of my passions that I will describe shortly.

I need to pause here and mention a few things about my strange autobiography. I have described my youth, education, travels and family which by themselves were a full life so I should have died with Ella in 2031. But I was still young with a lot of life still to live. I can't explain why but my young body and soul just reset, renew and start the natural aging process over again mirroring and repeating a normal person's stages in life. It was quite strange because, as I gradually discovered, repeating and extending life's early natural stages in excess made them conspicuously pointless. But it was an exciting time so I just went with the flow. For now my passions took over my being and I spent the next 85 years trying to satisfy them, like John Stuart Mill's satisfied pig. After 2126, as you shall see, I pursued different more enduring passions with mixed results.

After a few years my life of anonymity in Burns came to an abrupt end when someone recognized me from the *New York Times* article. I quickly packed my bags, said goodbye to Stella and hitchhiked to San Francisco where I became an Epicurean. I did this kind of abrupt leaving often in life for the same reason.

San Francisco at that time was the Sodom and Gomorrah of America, the two notoriously sinful cities in antiquity described in the Old Testament that were destroyed by God with sulfur and fire for their wickedness and debauchery. Like them, San Francisco was a sea of human reproductive fluids being exchanged and any kind of sexual perversion could be had. It was ground one for an Epicurean although less populated than it used to be because many had migrated north due to the heat and smoke from global warming and forest fires. Ironically, I got a job at renamed Calhoun Securities Inc. as a neophyte broker to earn money.

Two of the seven deadly sins are gluttony and lust and I found myself pursuing both of them with a passion in San Francisco. When I started making money I gambled, went to horse races and ate at the finest restaurants. I was into food and excitement and any pleasure that could satisfy my appetites. But by far my worst passion was sensual pleasure. I felt lust and wanted sex. I am not sure why but it may have been Stella's small-town sexual appeal that ignited this passion. In any case I fell in with a group of young, loose and wild people, which was quite strange considering I was chronologically four times their age.

I must apologize here because what follows is quite graphic. I did not intend this to be a pornographic book but it would not be an honest autobiography without a description of my time in San Francisco. If you are morally uptight and easily offended you may want to skip the next couple of paragraphs.

The young group I fell in with had many beautiful and sexy young hormonally driven women eager for sex who paraded their bodies in revealing mini-skirts and tops all of which is irrelevant because they were usually naked. Sex with them was a paralyzing pleasure and our orgies were one long, delirious orgasm akin to temporary insanity. It was glorious to feel like a teenage boy again. I became a Casanova-like lothario who knew exactly how to seduce a woman. The formula was quite simple; look presentable, smile, be nice, listen, get close and let nature take her course. I seduced a lot of women with this formula. It was an orgasmic time of my life.

I was totally irresponsible and would often move to another sexual group if any problems like pregnancy or jealousy surfaced. You may censure me for being a callous old lecherous man but remember that even though I was more than one hundred chronologically I was in my early thirties biologically (I had only aged a couple of years) and that the young women were as eager as me for sex.

During these years of debauchery my conscience was assuaged by my favorite fifteenth-century philosopher, Desiderius Erasmus, whom I had studied at Oxford. I remembered much of his famous book *In Praise of Folly* had pitted passion against reason. As I saw it I was pursuing my passion for pleasure which for Erasmus is folly that ultimately brings happiness. I recalled that it would because he believed folly brings ignorance, thoughtlessness, forgetfulness of evil, hope of good and a dash of delight. Scorn, for example would be ignored because what isn't noticed isn't troublesome. The folly of mindlessly pursuing passionate sex for Erasmus is a spree that never ends, does not require any bothersome preparation and is available to all. I particularly took solace in his view that illusion will bring happiness because its price is low and it maintains ecstasy. It seemed the less I thought the more I enjoyed life.

But my passion for sex and this kind of thinking changed one day in 2057 when I was about 32. After an orgy, for the first time I felt completely empty. I felt no pleasure or satisfaction from the act because it was just more of the same. Remembering Ella, I also realized it was just more of the same because it was without love. Experience had taught me Erasmus was wrong and Epicures' dictum that at some point pleasure cannot be increased, only varied, was right. I came to realize that sexual pleasure itself is not an enduring source of happiness and my age of sensual pleasure abruptly came to an end.

I found it fascinating to study the last 700 years of human history, roughly the sixteenth through twenty-third centuries, because I witnessed some of it personally and much of it through OMNI. Before my time was the 1500s through 1950, my biologic era was from when I was born in 1950 to when I should have died in 2011, and after my era was 2012 to 2250 due to my altered aging genome. It was fascinating to observe the things that changed and those that did not. Most of the changes were in science, religion and earth and the constants were war and human nature.

Before my time, humans traveled in horse-driven carriages, during my biologic era in airplanes going 600 miles an hour and after my era they traveled in time. Before my time if you got cancer you died, during my era you got radiation and chemotherapy treatments and might live and after my era you got an over-the-counter nasal spray that altered you genes and your cancer was cured. Before my time you wrote someone a paper letter, during my era you called or e-mailed them and after my era with microchip implants you talked telepathically through thought. Before my time people worshiped the moon, during my era in 1969 Neil Armstrong walked on the moon and after my era humans lived on the moon. Before my time everyone was religious and believed in God, during my era science began to understand the mysteries religion wrongly explained and after my era everyone was secular. Before my time Nikolaus Otto invented the internal combustion engine, during my time earth's oil deposits were consumed to feed his engine and after my era his engine caused earth to get hot and largely uninhabitable.

John L. Bowman

War and human nature were two constants over those 700 years. Before my time 107 to 122 million people died in World Wars One and Two, during my era over 5 million died in the Korean and Vietnam Wars and after my era millions died in nuclear wars. Before my time you were either a man or a woman, during my era you could be either and after my era humans almost became unisex and extinct. As you shall see, the human race survived only because constant human nature forcefully reasserted itself and two distinct genders reemerged and again started reproducing.

I learned two things from my age of pleasure. First, Mill's satisfied pigs pursuing pleasure live meaningless, empty and solitary lives because there is no love in pleasure; pleasure becomes just more of the same and pleasure turns our focus inward. Second, I learned how much I missed my mom, the friends I grew up with, my wife Ella and my children. I missed my era.

So, I got fixed and started pondering what to do next.

CHAPTER 5

The Richest Man in the Grave

32-37
(2061-2080)

So, here I was in 2061 burned out from 19 years of sensual pleasure, 32 years old biologically, 111 chronologically, most of my historic family gone and living in San Francisco wondering what to do next.

I had been poor most of my life and had enjoyed the exciting risk-taking when I started my securities business in Portland in 2000. I did not know how much I was worth but with my house and securities perhaps around a million, so I thought about getting rich. I did not think getting rich was about avarice, another of the seven deadly sins, but rather about having some fun and making money. So, I decided to get rich which I pursued with a passion for the next nineteen years.

At that time the place to go to acquire wealth was the city of New York. It was the commercial and financial center of the world and housed the New York Stock Exchange, the biggest stock exchange in the world. For fun and because I was in no hurry I decided to drive there on the 130-year-old nostalgic highway then called Route 66. It was a 2,000-mile narrow interstate two-lane highway created in the 1920s connecting Los Angeles and Chicago that traversed the then rural heart of America through many now-extinct small towns. It was an American legend that started with the golden sands of California, skirted the Grand Canyon, bisected the flat southwest desert of Texas and Oklahoma and ended in the gritty streets of Chicago. It had been decommissioned in 1984 because the American Federal government paved some of it over with a freeway system beginning in 1957. I went to Los Angeles to find a car for the drive. I was lucky to find a jet black 84-year-old Pontiac Firebird Formula muscle car with only 560,000 miles. It had been perfectly restored, I bought it for $150,000 and set out for New York.

I felt free, alive and happy driving with the T-top open across the Mojave Desert in California, one of the driest places on the planet with an average of three inches of rainfall annually. It can go years without a drop. It wound through small towns with old blinking neon signs, rusty truck stops and faded motels—it was wonderfully kitschy Americana. My first night I stayed in the faded Palm Motel in Needles. It was torture because it was 100 degrees and the room had no air conditioning.

I was glad to be on 66 again in the cool morning when I picked up a wanderlust hitchhiker in the middle of nowhere. His name was Garrett, he had no last name, he was young, had long hair, was wearing shorts, sandals and a ragged T-shirt that said *Diogenes is Cool*. He turned out to be quite interesting-as I discovered he was remarkably resourceful, exuberant and funny. I asked him where he was going and he said nowhere in particular because his philosophy of life was to travel for travel's sake—the journey was more important than the destination. This precipitated an extended philosophic conversation with Garrett about the meaning of life, the nature of knowledge and the relative merits of Plato, Aristotle, Kant and Hume.

Along the way a truck in front of us spilled some hops on the road, I pulled to the side and Garrett eagerly gathered them along with a nearby dead squashed raccoon. With this windfall that night camping Garrett produced a very good stew he called roadkill and eventually brewed a tasty lager he called asphalt.

Together we drove through Arizona and skirted the Grand Canyon happily singing the1946 hit song "Get Your Kicks on Route 66," through the land of enchantment New Mexico past ancient Mesa Verde cliff dwellings and along the 200-mile flat pancake desert of Texas. I dropped Garrett off in Amarillo, Texas because he had tuberculosis and had to go into isolation for six months. For fun I went back in OMNI to see what happened to Garrett. After recuperating from tuberculosis he became a Shaman Priest, later the founder and spiritual leader of the ancient wild Burning Man Festival in the Black Rock Desert of Nevada and later got rich selling t-shirts with catchy sayings.

Alone I continued on into Oklahoma, the origin of what was once a dust bowl famine. It was from here in the early 1900s in America that many people on the verge of starvation began migrating west to California for better lives on the very road I was taking east for the same reason.

In the middle of the desert near the Oklahoma-Texas border I saw a car on the side of the road and stopped to help. A hysterical young woman screamed her young daughter had just been bitten by a venomous sidewinder and was dying. The girl was ashen, convulsing and whimpering in a fetal position. The next hospital was in Clinton, about 50 miles away, so I said get in and buckle up. I fired the Firebird 400 V8 with its 200-horsepower engine, put the pedal to the metal, cranked quickly through the four speeds and quickly hit 140 miles per hour. The Firebird was humming. Like Commander Cody's song "Hot Rod Lincoln," I was *passing cars like they were standing still, the lines in the road looked like dots and the no longer hysterical woman beside me was white as a ghost.* I passed a state cop in the blink of an eye and before I knew it I had a trail of 5 or 6 state, county and local police cars chasing me. I got to Clinton in about 20 minutes, screamed through traffic to the hospital and came to a screeching stop in their emergency entrance. The woman ran in with her now-comatose daughter and I lit a cigarette as the police surrounded me with unholstered guns. I told them what happened, one cop went in and talked with the mother and doctor and came back and said my story was true. The doctor said that the antivenin was given just in time and the girl would live. She would have died if it had been a minute later. The cops shook my hand, slapped me on the back and let me go.

I went back once with OMNI and visited these women. I learned that they had been looking for me for years to thank me so I flew in my private Cessna fifth generation Citation Impulse 4000 jet to Oklahoma City where they were living and introduced myself. Both cried while passionately hugging me and the now young woman mother herself thanked me for saving her life. It was one of the most touching and gratifying experience of my life.

Back on the road I skirted Kansas, the setting of an old movie, *The Wizard of Oz* and blasted through the hilly Ozark Highlands and Meramec Caverns where ancient cowboy bandit Jessie James hid out in Missouri. Civilization reemerged when I got to crowded St. Louis. I passed through Springfield the home of one of America's most celebrated presidents, Abraham Lincoln, and arrived in bustling Chicago. Route 66 ended here so I took the now-decrepit old I-90 and I-80 on to New York. When I got there I parked my Firebird on a street while I got something to eat and it was quickly stolen. I really missed my old car and through OMNI discovered a teenager had stolen it, crashed it, it was sold to a wrecking yard that melted it down into metal which was sold to American Home Kitchenware Company. My wonderful Firebird was reincarnated as home cookware throughout America.

New York was bigger than life. It was the hotbed of American action that had been made famous by American composer Leonard Bernstein's *America* that celebrated America's early strength and vibrancy. It was also richer than I imagined, with money in private equity funds, mutual funds, Fortune 500 companies, real estate investment trusts and untold wealthy families.

I wasted no time, I went to my bank that held my investment account in Portland, transferred $200,000 to my new checking account, rented an expensive apartment in midtown Manhattan, bought six Gucci suits and went to dinner at Le Bernardin. After getting settled I went to my old company Calhoun Securities, now CS Securities and applied for a job as an account executive. I was quickly hired and began succeeding beyond imagination because I knew everything about securities and the company. One day my manager rebuked me for calling on another broker's client, which was against company policy to which I calmly said company policy does not prohibit a broker from calling on other broker's clients on general matters. I knew this because I had written the company's Policies and Procedures manual. He never bothered me again.

I worked like a madman on a mission adding wealthy clients, investing money and executing stock puts, calls and straddles. I ascended the ranks and quickly became the jealous rival of Thad Collins and his minion Henry Blank, the firm's top producers. I called them Yuk Yuk brokers because they got business with funny stories and laughs. Henry, who had a lisp, would do superficial Thad's dirty work like rifling my files. I was amused and the rivalry did not last long because my hard work, talent and knowledge overwhelmed their pretentiousness.

Working at CS Corporation was exciting but bereft of intellectual thought. It was all about money. I had enjoyed my classes in philosophy at Oxford so one day I walked down to Greenwich Village in Lower Manhattan to 240-year-old New York University and enrolled in a philosophy class. I loved the class and spent the next ten years leaving the office midday, walking to the university in the colorful fall, cold winter and resurgent spring taking philosophy classes. I was an anomaly with my pinstriped suit amongst the jeans and torn t-shirts of the twenty-year-olds but I did not care. I once took OMNI back and watched myself after a class sundering through Washington Square Park deep in thought and remembered how excited I was then having learned something new and profound. I remember reading and trying to understand Kant's *Critique of Pure Reason*, being elated with Spinoza's *Ethics* and his reasoning for pantheism and my philosophy of religion class where the professor asked us how we could possibly discuss religion when everyone defines it differently. I was having so much fun I decided to pursue a doctorate in philosophy and NYU readily accepted me because I had a BA in philosophy from Oxford, even though it was a hundred years earlier (they thought it was a typographical error). I was given a rigorous course of study and assigned a major professor, Bill Engelsome.

My relationship with Bill was an adventure in itself. He was cranky, brilliant, fearsome, caring, sixtyish, heavyset, usually bent over, abrupt and mostly unkempt. Above all he was funny and told his students to get a good grade they must have humor also. Because he was legally blind in one eye he would bend his balding head down and cock it to a side in such a way that his one good eye would get an unnerving bead on me—it was like being examined by the Hunchback of Notre Dame. He had a fearsome reputation and undergraduate students were terrified of him, like an evil god from below. In one class Bill entered red-faced and irritated because he had been reading a batch of undergraduate philosophy papers and contemptuously said, "If you want to torture someone make them read undergraduate students' philosophy papers!" One day I e-mailed Bill asking for a meeting and in jest signed it Murphy, thinking of Murphy's Law if anything can go wrong it will, because I was having a bad day. When I arrived I said "Calhoun is here" and Bill yelled "get out" and I said "but you said I could come" and he said "I said Murphy could come not Calhoun!" So went our relationship.

Over time, we became great friends and would often go to a campus bar and discuss philosophy, argue politics and laugh. One day I told Bill my story of aging and that I was over a hundred years old. He is this only person who immediately believed me because he was a Buddhist scholar who believed in reincarnation and said it was about time someone visited him from the past.

I spent eight years with taskmaster Bill, intensely studying, reading and writing my dissertation "Stoicism, Enkrasia and Happiness," and was awarded a PhD in philosophy in 2080. When I was done Bill and I hugged goodbye and I moved on.

It was strange to work in my old company where a photo of me was on the wall with the inscription *Reggie Calhoun, founder and president emeritus in abstentia*. I decided to regain control of the company and began a high-stakes legal battle with the board of directors claiming I was Reggie's son. Everyone agreed I looked like him, but I could produce no death certificate or will proving my case.

However, I could prove that I was the Reggie Calhoun that owned the mysterious majority-stock-owner trust of the company that I had set up long ago. I won the case so at 32 I took ownership of the multi-million-dollar international CS Corporation. Thad Collings and Henry Blank quickly departed.

It was amazing how fast my wealth accumulated. I could hardly keep track of it. A large salary, commissions, profit and dividends from CS and the many Fortune 500 companies I acquired through leveraged buyouts, rent from real estate investments poured in and I got very rich. By 2070, when I was about 35, I was worth around $100 million, which generated an income of about $6 million a year, $500,000 a month or $17,000 a day!

My life became unreal, decadent and exciting in New York with a lot of strange people. One of my clients was crazy Ivan Zhukov, a Russian immigrant who swindled millions from investors in a mutual fund ponzi scheme and once, with no money of his own, finagled to build-to-suit the headquarters for the United Nations on vacant waterfront property owned by the New York Port Authority. Another was charlatan investor Jeffrey Erskine who amassed wealth through manipulation of stocks and used it to buy fabulous houses, private islands, yachts, jets and illegal young girls.

I began questioning a society built on wealth because it corrupts and detaches people from reality. Society in New York was a string of sophisticated, jaded, empty and decedent parties where who you knew was all that mattered. The real concept of gender lost its meaning because most people were homosexual, lesbian, gay, bisexual or transgender. It was like San Francisco times ten without heterosexuality. Everyone was effeminate and being called masculine was an insult. Both sexes had forgotten the purpose of their genitals. The ideal beautiful woman was an emaciated skeleton; an unhealthy starving person was beautiful.

Wealth also made New York an ironic bubble detached from the real world where, on one hand, it was businesslike vibrant with one foot in reality, and the other decadent with the other foot in never-never land. Unlike the rest of rural America with its ethic of self-reliance, the New Yorker would quickly die in nature because they were accustomed to being provided for. They had no clue where their food, shelter and electricity came from. Surplus wealth had enabled an unreal socialistic place focused entirely on needs so often lauded by their strange hyper-partisan now defunct *New York Times* newspaper.

Living in New York made me think about this new political phenomenon of socialism because New York was its epicenter in America. America was founded on capitalism that embraced freedom, Emerson's self-reliant individual and the private control of the means of production. It unleashed the able and created unprecedented wealth. It made America great. Bentham's serpent winding socialism came later, embraced collectivism, fostered other-reliance with its emphasis on need and championed the state control of the means of production. It began with a Frenchman Saint-Simon in the 1700s and expanded by German fire-eater Karl Marx in the 1800s and revolutionary Russian Vladimir Lenin in the 1900s. It infected America in the early 1900s and advanced for two hundred years under the political banner of Progressivism. The contest between the eagle and snake got quite nasty after 2080.

Around 2075 my $100 million had escalated to a billion and by 2080 at 36 it exceeded $250 billion. I set up a private equity company, RC Holdings, LLC and consolidated my portfolio. I even owned the Caribbean nation of Granada, which I bought at a bargain. I also hired a young investment broker, Albert Martin, who had recently graduated from Harvard, to manage the assets. I had become the richest man in America and one of the richest in the world and could buy anything I desired including expensive estates, the biggest yachts and the most beautiful women. I was the envy of many but I felt empty. When I could have anything, things became less valuable and nothing was worth having. It turned out that the more money I got life became less meaningful. It did not matter if I was the richest man in the grave.

I could not help remembering from Oxford Tolstoy's character Pierre in *War and Peace* who came to believe that the satisfaction of our basic needs is the highest form of happiness. The simple enjoyment of eating when you are hungry, drinking when you are thirsty, sleeping when you are tired and keeping warm when you are cold. A surfeit of luxury, such as pleasure and wealth, takes all the joy out of satisfying these basic needs because by destroying the need you lose the desire for these simple things.

I had had fun as a securities broker and getting rich, but like pleasure I tired of accumulating money and the pressure-cooker environment seemed to accelerate my aging process. So, I decided to do something else with my life, gave $50 billion to the Oregon Health and Science University in Portland with the sole purpose of finding a cure for cancer and prepared to take off. OHSU was stunned with such a massive gift and wheels turned. I enjoyed going back in OMNI years later to watch what happened to my money. OHSU built new facilities, hired an army of talented medical scientists and spent many billions on a few promising gene treatments. It is complicated but their research teams identified over 200 hybrid genes that affect sections of DNA that cause cells to go into hyper-growth. It turned out that the culprit was a mutation in the BRCA1 gene that would damage the growth control p53 gene. They discovered how to genetically repair p53 with an injection and later a nasal spray to repair the damage and presto facto, just like the Rockefeller Foundation had done in 1914 with Yellow Fever, they found a treatment and eradicated the greatest killer of humans, cancer.

While living in New York I was struck by how people revered the wealthy. These old-family famous people enjoyed prestige just because of their name. At a cocktail party if someone said they had lunch with Jay Rockefeller's grandson it would hush and all ears would turn. So, I decided to gain prestige through fame by becoming an actor.

CHAPTER 6

Celebrity

37-42
(2081-2100)

The epicenter for acting in 2081 was still the tinsel town in southwestern America called Hollywood that was ironically named after a conservative Dutch settlement in Ohio, so that is where I went. My Cesena landed at Los Angeles International Airport at seven in the morning. I put an ad in *Plane and Pilot Magazine* (and sold it a month later for $12 million) and grabbed a cab to Hollywood. The first thing I noticed was how much Los Angeles had changed since my last visit. It was very hot. The heavy air smelled like a forest fire and there were far fewer cars on the road because many people had migrated north. Fortunately the movie studios were still churning out movies. It was perfect. In 2081 I was still relatively young at 37 but my appearance had changed enough so I was no longer recognized from the *New York Times* article, and I was rich. I spent the next 19 years trying to become a famous actor in order to achieve prestige.

The cab dropped me off on Sunset Boulevard in the heart of Hollywood. Aimlessly I wandered into nearby Laurel Park and sat on a bench to ponder what to do next. After a bit of introspection I noticed this disheveled unshaven gloomy-looking middle age man talking to himself sitting next to me. I thought he was mentally ill until he began talking at me making sense. He said his name was Corey Michaels, he learned that morning his wife was divorcing him, he had to move out of his house with no place to live, he might lose his job in the movie business and was sitting here because he was depressed and didn't know what to do. Our conversation deepened. I told him my story, we laughed, we went to the local pub and drank too many beers and ended up renting an apartment together just off Sunset Boulevard. Unbeknownst to me I had befriended one of the most complicated, interesting and memorable people I ever met in my long life.

Corey liked to gamble and owed money to many people, including the mob. One day two heavyset menacing-looking guys in black showed up at our door, drug Corey into a corner, put a silenced.38 muzzle in this mouth and whispered "pay or die." Corey said kill me. They left and we moved to another nearby apartment. Corey was also under suspicion by the police for murder. A young starlet had mysteriously disappeared and he was the last person seen with her. The detectives were not as impressive as the mob thugs. It later turned out she had taken off for a tryst with a young actor. One day out of the blue his two angry adult daughters showed up and yelled at him for cheating on their mom. He sat quietly because he loved his wife and children. I had noticed that women were attracted to him and he dallied but was never lecherous.

I learned much more about Corey living together and drinking beer every night at the Lost Property Bar. He was an irresponsible diabetic with a heart condition, an off- and on-again alcoholic, a superstitious Hindu who believed in an afterlife, very eccentric and spoke with an engaging aristocratic English accent. Remarkably, unlike most people in Hollywood he was not pretentious or egotistic and his favorite quips were "shit happens" and "I have prejudices, but they are correct." He also loved to quote Sophocles' aphorism "it is a mistake to wait to the evening to see how splendid the day has been," due to his joie de vivre. He was just refreshingly fun.

It was only later that I learned why women, and in particular starlets,were attracted to him. It turned out that my friend Corey was a powerful studio mogul, president of Universal Studios, one of the biggest studios at that time, and had produced many successful films. He had a canny sense in his business because he was imaginative, smart, intuitively knew people and recognized talent. The women wanted parts to become famous actresses and Corey was their ticket. Fortuitously, he ended up being my ticket.

I quickly discovered it is impossible to break into acting in Hollywood but I was lucky. Corey first steered me to the Stella Adler Academy of Acting, then made a call to the William Morris Agency who changed my name to Hugh Dangerton and arranged my first acting job, which was an anonymous stormtrooper in a remake of the earlier famous *Star Wars*. My next gig was a forgettable victim that got stabbed by zombies in a horror film called *The Wrath of Zombies*. I began thinking acting is the wrong way to gain prestige because all actors do is mime, which was a pretty empty thing to do. In the last of a few supporting roles in a Hallmark movie I played an urban cowboy who moves to the country and falls in love with a simple local girl. I thought little of the movie until *Hollywood Life* favorably mentioned me in a review. In spite of my obvious mediocre talent the article said I was handsome with my long red hair, sexually attractive, warm, dashing, insouciant and likeable with a bigger-than-life persona. I thought this is the kind of thing that could give someone an ego.

Apparently, I had tremendous screen presence—one that magically attracted attention. For some reason my features were magnified on celluloid that made me an irresistible and compelling character. Like that, my dead-end acting career took off and my path to prestige opened, but along a very strange path.

Acting is an unusual profession. Unlike most jobs it takes place on an artificial set intended to create illusion. It is populated by egotistic striving people which makes for a dog-eat-dog distrustful atmosphere. Actors' relations are rife with jealousy, intrigue, subterfuge and sabotage. One jealous actress exposed her breasts while filming a movie in order to one-up another actress. In addition to the constant gossip magnified by the tabloid celebrity press there was ubiquitous easy promiscuity with trysts, liaisons and orgies. I avoided these because I knew about empty unsatisfiable passion. In spite of this I noticed that talent always rose in the end and, along with culture, inevitably brought fame. Talent became fame when it met some cultural need. Long-gone actors like masculine John Wayne gained fame in times of danger like during war because people yearned for security, and others like saucy Mae West got it in times of peace because people wanted pleasure. I found myself at one such nexus due to my strong masculine character and increasing civil unrest.

Corey gave me my big break. Universal was casting another remake of an earlier popular film *The Great Escape* starring long-dead actor Steve McQueen. They were looking for an actor with his persona—a cool, irresistible, confident and courageous who remains calm and thinking in dangerous situations and knew how to ride a vintage motorcycle. Corey steered them to me. I got the role, nailed it, the film was a tremendous success and overnight I was ushered into the ephemeral world of celebrity. Fictitious Hugh Dangerton became a household name. I started getting massive fan mail from people I did not know, groupies began following me and I was recognized in awe everywhere. I did it, I was a celebrity, I was famous and I now had prestige, but deep down I felt guilty because I did not think I deserved it for just miming.

Looking back I now realize that during my years in Los Angeles I was witnessing the beginning of an end. At first I thought little about the political gridlock, increasing incivility, demonstrations and occasional riots and considered it the usual human occasional inclination to violence. Corey thought it was just kids having fun but as events unfolded I saw something more ominous. Alarmingly the violence increased, protests sometimes resulted in street gun fights, wild shouting people were running everywhere with weapons, barricades were erected and freeways blocked. The police were overwhelmed and people started killing people. Unbeknownst to me at the time I was watching the breakdown of civil society and the American Civil War that began in 2090.

The conflagration quickly escalated. Individual states stopped cooperating with each other and the coastal states began to square off with the central states. The American central federal government tried to stem the conflict but was impotent because most states refused to help. Bloody regional battles erupted in flashpoints like Ely, Nevada, Columbus, Ohio and Charlotte, North Carolina. In Los Angeles riots and anarchy reigned and it became quite dangerous so I bought a wicked-looking M4 Carbine Commando with a M203 grenade launcher that I brandished often to protect myself. The studios shut down, electricity disappeared, water was cut off and the grocery store shelves went empty, so I decided to get out and headed north to our family property in Oregon.

I went to the now-abandoned studio, took the vintage motorcycle and headed north on I-5 just like I had 100 years earlier after my time in Mexico. It was eerily quiet riding up I-5 with no cars or people until I got to Weed, California near the Oregon border where a menacing-looking military tank unit blocked the freeway. I veered off on Highway 97 which was surprisingly clear until I got to another military blockade at Warm Springs. I went off-road, heading west through the eastern Oregon desert on the bike. It was exhilarating, riding through the virgin desert at night alone like Ted Simon who had written *Jupiter Travels* about his riding a motorcycle around the world. I remembered how he had described traveling through the North African Sarah Desert where there are no roads—rather only "a way" to some destination. Eventually I ran into Highway 26 which took me over the Cascade Mountains to Mt. Hood and Arrah Wanna.

Riding in to the family retreat, it felt as verdant and peaceful as I remembered, much like it had 90 years earlier when Ella and I had escaped Portland and the great earthquake. When I arrived I found about twenty strange people of all ages alarmed, armed and curious— they did not know why a famous actor like Hugh Dangerton was here. It occurred to me that Arrah Wanna was no longer in my family. It was a tense moment with each of us not knowing what to think of the other. I said my name is Reggie Calhoun and this property was in my family for more than a hundred years. They looked at me astonished until one very curious old woman asked about my wife. I was taken aback but said my wife had been Ella and I described the big house where we had raised our six children in Portland. The old woman screamed, cried, ran over and hugged me and said, "HI, DAD"! It was my youngest daughter, Ella, now 90 years old! Arrah Wanna was still in my family after 200 years and these were my descendants, still using the property and escaping the civil war. I couldn't believe it. Along with Ella I met my son Edward along with a host of their children and grandchildren.

There were lots of questions and I had a lot of explaining to do. I told them of my slowed aging, that I was 38 biologically but nearly 150 chronologically, and the events of my life. They were rapturously interested and wanted to know more, especially about their ancestors. My son John had died young but had children, one of whom was 60-year-old John II, who I met, as well as Maude's, Pete's, Ella's and Edward's children and their children. I told them how their ancient aunt Sybil had disappeared on the Pacific Crest Trail in the early 2000s, about the personalities of their parents like Maude and Pete and the wonderful character of their matriarch Ella. I was struck with the similar appearance, temperament and gestures these descendants had with their ancestors. I thought to myself that this is an unprecedented occurrence when a long-dead ancestor actually gets to live with and get to know their descendants.

After about six months the reunion came to an abrupt end when we learned that our country America was no more. The coastal states had defeated the interior states in a bloody civil war but were unable to occupy the vast center, so America had Balkanized into four new countries. The Northeast had become The Socialist Atlantic States of America, or SASA, the Southeast was now the long-desired Confederate States of America, or CSA, the Center states were the United States of America, or USA, and the West Coast states had become the Socialistic Pacific States of America, or SPSA. I was dismayed that history's longest experiment with democracy had failed. American Founding Father Benjamin Franklin had said we have given you a republic and it is up to you to keep it, but apparently we couldn't. A one-of-a-kind form of government that originated on July 4, 1776 promising life, liberty and happiness had died 324 years later in July 2100. Early American composer Leonard Bernstein's lively and vibrant America was no longer.

Much has been written on why America ended. Some pundits claimed it was due to two incompatible worldviews, one of individuality, capitalism and objectivism and the other of collectivism, socialism and subjectivism. Some attributed it to excessive wealth and the luxury and immorality it brought like ancient Rome. Philosophers attributed it to the inexorable clash between the ideals of freedom, justice and equality and some legal scholars cited the loss of the rule of law and equal treatment under the law. Others blamed the very nature of democracy itself because it brought de Toqueville's tyranny of the majority. All cited intolerant ideology as a source. Personally, I think it was due to the timeless war between the rich haves and the poor have-nots, but what do I know.

That period of my life taught me two things. The first was to appreciate tolerance, civility and stable society. Civility is like health—when you have it you take it for granted and when you lose it all you can think about is getting it back. The second was that prestige, like pleasure and wealth, is an empty goal. I had achieved prestige, I was a famous actor, I got my name on the Hollywood Walk of Stars and I got an Oscar. What I found was prestige brings an army of pretentious and envious admiring sycophants who do not honor you for your character but only because you are known. It occurred to me that true esteem is only earned through right character and selfless deeds. Out of curiosity I used OMNI to find out what happened to Corey but he had mysteriously disappeared never to be found. It was probably the mob.

After months with my ancestors at Arrah Wanna I decided it was time to move on so I said goodbye, hopped on my vintage motorcycle, slung my M4 Carbine over my shoulder and headed west on Highway 26. After all I had been through I wanted to escape civilization and become invisible so I headed to the unpopulated Oregon coast. It was a torturous ride because there was chaos and destruction everywhere due to the civil war. Portland looked like a war zone, much of it had burned and ragged casualties were everywhere. I rode on to Astoria, Oregon at the coast, pulled into a marina and spotted this breath-taking classic two-masted 40' schooner at the wharf with a for sale sign. I parked the bike and while admiring it an old man approached and asked if I was interested. He said his name was Bill Weatherspoon, he owned the boat and would be happy to give me a tour.

It turned out to be an elegant old-style mahogany-appointed yacht with a large comfortable living room, a well-stocked library, three comfortable bedrooms with showers, a modern galley and spacious aft deck. It also looked in excellent condition with a spotless engine room. It was like the perfect luxurious comfortable retreat and isolated oasis away from civilization that I was looking for.

Bill and I went to the local Mariners Bar in downtown Astoria to work out a deal. We drank and talked and I learned a lot about him. His name was Bill Weatherspoon, he was about 70, he had been married and divorced and was surprisingly erudite—it turned out he had graduated from Oxford in 2050, about 80 years after me. He listened intently as I told him my story of slowed aging, OMNI and my life's adventures, including the *New York Times* article and acting career. He said he was wondering why a famous actor was in Astoria and was surprised I was the individual in the article that he had read in a journalism class. I described some of my Oxford professors, whom he had only heard about. Bill was educated, interesting, funny and fluent in French with a very mild personality set off with erratic white hair and very bushy eyebrows who always wanted a motorcycle. At one point in our conversation he looked pensive and said his beloved 25-year-old daughter Hester had died in the civil war which had caused a deep sadness. I told him I wanted to buy his boat and sail around the world but did not know how to sail. It turned out Bill was an old salt—he had spent a good part of his life sailing, was a master sailor and said he would teach me if he could come along. The boat was worth millions but due to the economic chaos of the civil war there were no buyers so he sold it to me for $50,000 and the motorcycle, along with his promise to teach me to sail. We took a couple of days to stock the boat and store the bike and then set sail together westward out into the vast Pacific Ocean. I kept the carbine.

It was one of the richest experiences of my life. I first learned how to sail from Bill. It was a rigorous month learning about navigation, the azimuth and celestial objects, compass, the Global Positioning System, tacking, leeward and windward, the mainsail, jib and spinnaker and how to trim them along with the rigging and halyards. In time I became quite proficient at sailing which I did with pleasure traveling the globe's oceans. In the evenings Bill and I would sit comfortably in the aft deck as dusk descended on the open ocean drinking five-star Mattix brandy, intensely discussing everything including politics, philosophy, history and literature. It was a time when my intellectual curiosity was aroused and challenged. Sometimes I would talk of Ella, my ancient family and dead children and Bill would go quiet and then start reminiscing about his beloved daughter Hester. We got to know everything about each other and would laugh at the strange reversal of our roles—I was in my early forties but had lived longer than Bill. During those magic nights I came about as close to another human being as possible.

We docked in Hawaii, restocked and headed out again to sea heading west. I was glad this time I could leave freely, unlike the time in 1970 when I had been dragged back to the tramp steamer after having jumped ship in Honolulu. We spent months on the open ocean sailing to Tahiti, restocked there and then sailed toward Vanuatu in the deep South Pacific. This period of my life was not only interesting but the most tranquil. I loved the tropical, sultry, sunny and sudden warm torrential rains on the open seas away from the rush of civilization. It was magical at night with the stars feeling free, one with nature and at peace with the world. The globe was my oyster and life was good.

From Vanuatu we sailed to Malang, Indonesia where we again refueled and restocked the boat. In the busy marketplace we were warned of pirates who prey on foreigners. Bill and I thought little of it until a couple of hours out of port about a mile offshore two speed boats filled with shouting pirates started chasing us with guns blazing. Bill took the helm and gunned the engine and I went aft with my M4 Carbine Commando M203 grenade launcher. As they closed Bill started swearing at them in French and I sent off a few grenades that blew one of the boats out of the water and then sprayed the other with bullets. The stunned pirates turned and ran and Bill and I had a Mattix brandy to toast our victory.

Our journey went smoothly until the Maldives off the southern tip of India when we ran into a gale. The sky had turned a menacingly dark and the ocean began churning. Before we knew it, we were in a full-scale storm with 90-mile winds and 40-foot waves. I quickly retreated below deck and held on for life as the boat was tossed like a rag doll for what seemed like eternity. I remember thinking I am going to die. On one violent roll I hit my head on a cabinet that knocked me out. When I awoke I staggered to the deck to a calm sea but no Bill. I frantically searched the boat but he was gone. He had been washed overboard during the tempest. All I could do was grieve at the loss of my old friend.

Alone, sad and somewhat disoriented I continued on across the Indian Ocean to Madagascar. It had been a long time at sea when I sailed into the northern port city of Mahajanga, Madagascar, docked and walked their palm-lined waterfront esplanade and sat alone on a bench thinking of Bill and pondering life. Sitting among the noisy food carts I realized how pointless the desire for prestige had been and thought about what I wanted to do next. I picked up an international edition of *USA Today* and was struck with the headline *NUCLEAR WAR!* While I had been at sea, nuclear war had broken out and over fifteen million people had died. I could hardly believe it.

I recalled my thought that worthiness comes from right character and selfless deeds, it occurred to me the way to become worthy would be through the acquisition of power. I wondered if I had been a powerful American leader whether I could have prevented the civil war. I decided I wanted to see if I could help the world avoid further nuclear wars—whether I could make a difference. So, in 2102 I abandoned my boat and caught a plane to Washington, D.C., which was the home of the United Nations.

CHAPTER 7

Cynicism

42-48
(2101-2125)

I first landed in New York and was asked by Customs my nationality, I said American and showed them my ragged passport and the official asked which America. I suddenly realized I had landed in the new Socialistic Atlantic States of America. They gave me a six-month visa and said I must establish a country of residence if I wanted to stay. Thus began what turned out to be one of the most painful, ironic, famous, notorious and wise time of my life.

I caught a cab and said I wanted to go to the offices of RC Holdings, LLC which was on Wall Street. The cabbie said they had moved long ago to the very old but prestigious Freedom Tower on Fulton Street. It turned out that my company had expanded to the top five floors of the 104-story tower in about 17,000 sq. ft. and was famous enough for a cabbie to know. In rumpled clothes I took the elevator to the 104th floor and said to the skeptical receptionist that I wanted to see the manager of the fund. She asked if I had an appointment and I said no, just tell him Reggie Calhoun wants to see him. Shortly now-45-year-old Albert Martin cautiously walked out, recognized me even though I was only 43 and to everyone's astonishment exclaimed "Mr. Calhoun, welcome back!" It turned out that Albert had done a superb job managing the fund by shifting assets to real estate when the civil war broke out, held steady during the nuclear exchanges and was in the process of returning to equities due to stabilized markets. The fund had grown to 250 billion. I congratulated Albert for doing a great job, said transfer one million to my checking account, and headed for Washington DC with more money than anyone on the planet.

Ancient American President Woodrow Wilson's League of Nations created in response to World War One in 1914 had changed to the United Nations in 1945. It had been located in New York on 18 acres with a general assembly building, a court of justice and a 39-story skyscraper built in the late 1940s by my former client Ivan Zhukov. It had been an idealistic world entity with little power until the horrific nuclear exchanges convinced everyone an overarching world government was necessary. Scared, political leaders quickly surrendered their sovereign power to the United Nations, it changed its name to the United Nations of Humankind or UNH and, because it needed more room, moved to recently vacated Washington DC. When I landed in Washington, I was entering the power center of the world. For me the place was exciting, awesome and fearful.

The nuclear exchanges that enabled the UNH were inevitable. German Otto Hahn had discovered nuclear fission in 1938 and American German Robert Oppenheimer made and exploded one in Alamogordo, New Mexico in 1945. Later that year America detonated two of them over Hiroshima and Nagasaki Japan which ended World War Two. Humans had opened Pandora's Box, the technology spread and nuclear arms proliferated. Over the next 150 years there were many close calls such as the 1962 Cuban Missile crisis, but the closest occurred in 2030 when a terrorist atomic bomb almost exploded in Boston, Massachusetts that would have killed ten million people. My now-extinct country was intent on revenge, discovered that it was the Islamic country of Iran that planted it with the intention of destroying "the Great Satan" and came within a whisker of turning their culture into glass. In hindsight America had been powerful stabilizing presence that prevented Armageddon but when it failed in 2100 a chaotic vacuum ensued that freed the nuclear Pandora.

In 2101 while I was happily at sea all hell had broken loose. In May both Pakistan and India had nuked military targets in the disputed Kashmir Valley killing three million, in September Islamic extremist Iran fired a nuke at Israel that was intercepted and Israel responded by nuking Tehran killing nine million and in November North Korea nuked a South Korean warship in the Yellow Sea and South Korea responded by nuking Pyongyang killing three million. Within seven months fifteen million people were incinerated.

During my political career I visited many of these devastated areas. They were gray, barren, uninhabited and lifeless areas like the surface of the moon. I was told that the temperature at the core of a nuclear blast briefly reaches those of the interior of the sun or about one hundred million degrees Celsius. The blast obliterates everything followed by firestorms, shock waves, electromagnetic pulses and radiation. Later in life I used OMNI to see downtown Hiroshima on August 5, 1945 at 8:15 am when the first atomic bomb exploded. The sidewalk was crowded with people going to work, it was a warm and clear morning and then suddenly brilliant whiteness, surprised faces that were instantly gone, hurricane winds and blindness due to swirling debris. I moved OMNI to a couple of days later thirty miles out of town and saw thousands of people dying agonizing radiation deaths. They were burned, blistered, scorched, vomiting and writhing from their burns dying along with others who would later die from radiation poisoning that had mutated their cells, causing cancer. It was horrific and one of the most painful things to watch in my life. With this I resolved to become a UNH politician to prevent this kind of mindless slaughter in the future.

When I got to the International Willard hotel in Washington there was an urgent message to call my granddaughter Ella. I called her and crying she said her mother had died of pancreatic cancer. My youngest daughter Ella had died. She also said Edward, my youngest son had also passed recently from heart disease, along with a few of my grandchildren. She also mentioned a few of her children and their cousins who were sick that I did not know. My spirit sank, at age 43 all of my parental family was dead, all my friends were dead, all of my family with Ella were dead and some of my grandchildren had died and I did not even know the names my great-grandchildren. It was the end of my biologic family, end of my era of life and I felt quite alone.

I was also beginning to feel the effects of aging. The first thing I noticed was the onset of CRS, or "can't remember shit." My mind was not as quick as it used to be and I started forgetting things. I had been asked to a political dinner party and the next day mentioned to a woman I kind of knew that I had been at a wonderful dinner party the night before. The woman said "Hugh, you were at my house for dinner, I was your hostess." I was embarrassingly speechless. The second was a surprise: I started getting clumsy. In my first campaign for office I was pacing back and forth giving a speech and fell off the dais. I climbed back on the platform, muttered "damn," and pretended it did not happen—after all I was over 150 years old.

It was 2102 when I was 43 biologically and 152 chronologically when I began my political career. Washington had changed. The American capitol building had become the United Nations Congress of Humankind, the Supreme Court building The World Court of Humankind, the Lincoln Memorial the Liberator of Humankind and the Pentagon the UNH World Military Authority. The Washington Memorial had been torn down because it was irrelevant and the White House had been painted brown and renamed The President's House because most of the world was colored. It was a quasi-democracy with voting and legislative, judicial and executive branches except the executive branch's president, then held by Japan's Ito Harari, had exceptional powers, and an overarching Security Council that could veto anything consisting of China, Russia, the four new American countries and the European Union which had replaced Great Britain and France, for a total of seven. It was the first true world government of humankind.

To get elected and satisfy my visa requirement I needed a country of residence so I headed to my old state Oregon which was now part of the Socialistic Pacific States of America. I found a troubled poor country playing out the eternal war between the rich and poor. I used my wealth to fund a campaign staff and buy advertising, trafficked on my reputation as charismatic motorcycle riding actor Hugh Dangerton and promised a better future through free enterprise because it would raise all boats. At one of my first speeches pacing back and forth concentrating on an important point I tripped on a microphone wire and again fell off the podium so everyone started calling me clumsy Hugh. To my surprise I became quite popular and was elected a Representative of SPSA to UNH.

I took my job seriously. I quietly encouraged industry to create jobs and wealth, sponsored State Farms for the poor, ill and mentally challenged, and quietly worked at mundane tasks like repairing the roads and bridges. I enjoyed the challenges, kept my head down and just kept working the problems. Over the years I got a reputation as a problem-solver who is frank, trustworthy, honest and clumsy. To my surprise, my constituents actually liked my quiet earnest ways and in 2110 elected me to be their Senator to UNH.

I had enjoyed my time as a local representative but as a long-time Senator I was dismayed at the intense internecine political warfare at the highest levels of world power. It was one of the most distasteful periods of my life. Most of my colleagues were power-hungry, humorless and cut-throat pretentious politicians who lied to their constituents, cut secret, back-room deals and advanced lobbyist clients' private interests to make money. I found high office politics not only ugly but very dangerous—assassinations were common. On the Senate floor for many years I sat next to Nagi Faziz who was a Senator from Nigeria. We talked often and I got to know well this man from the opposite side of the globe. He often talked fondly of his family and children back home and his country's problems. He was intensely interested in improving the welfare of his people. As our friendship blossomed Nagi and I would often go to dinner or play a round of golf together and he, like everyone else, would politely duck when I hit the ball. Nagi was struggling how to vote on a bill that pit his country's interests against all countries' interests. He voted for the universal solution, so on his next visit home his constituents thanked him for all his hard work with assassination. When we reassembled after holidays there were always a few vacant seats. To relieve the stress of politics one day on a whim I bought a Royal Enfield Himalayan touring bicycle and often left the fray and spent hours riding the Prince George region's back country roads to regain my sense of normalcy.

In 2117, at the end of my Senatorial term when I was biologically 47, I decided to quit politics but to my surprise and dismay was asked by the World Republican Party to go to their convention in Sydney, Australia as a possible candidate for Executive President of the UNH. It was a chaotic contentious convention with 9,000 delegates, demonstrations and back-room dealings. The real race for the presidency was between the reigning president Ito Harari and long-time Senator Herbert Long from the Confederate States of America. They deadlocked, the nominating committee started looking for a dark horse compromise and chose me. Desperate and wildly gesturing I told the conventioneers that I did not want the job, accidently knocked my water glass over and wacked the convention president next to me in the forehead, implored them not to vote for me and said if elected I would not serve. They thought anyone who is this clumsy and does not want the job that much must be the right one for it and nominated me.

I found myself in an ironic place. Had I pursued power to attain prestige or did I want to do some selfless, meaningful good in the world through right character such as preventing future nuclear wars and advancing stable civilization for all? I did not know the answer at that time so I put my head down, reluctantly campaigned for the job and won the worldwide election by a landslide. I was now the United Nations of Humankind's Executive President and the most powerful, prestigious and rich human on the planet with unrivaled fame.

To everyone's surprise I turned out to be a pretty good leader. I tackled many world problems but the pressing ones were nuclear weapons and the environment. We passed a law that banned all nuclear weapons, except a few reserved for the UNH, and methodically destroyed them all. Portions of the earth were gradually becoming uninhabitable so we passed a grinding series of laws limiting use of the internal combustion engine, limiting population growth and outlawing coal as a source of energy. I got a reputation for bravery. I was a hands-on leader who would go the source of the problem and work solutions. There were racial riots New York so I went to a Black caucus meeting amid rioting, took lots of heat from Black women, sent in the UNH security forces, stopped the riots and spent the night walking the streets. Another serious war erupted between India and Pakistan in my second year so I went to the battlefield in western India amongst bombs and bullets, called the two opposing politicians and generals together and said retreat or the UNH will no longer recognize your countries. Both quickly retreated. It was while adjudicating a violent dispute between Israel and Iran that I came the closest to being assassinated. During a speech in the war zone a young militant Islamic Jihadist angry because his Muslim country had become westernized raced to the podium, shot me through my right shoulder and was instantly subdued by security. People came to expect me to show up in areas of conflict and solve problems—and I did. I also got a reputation for blunt honesty. If there was a scandal, underhanded dealings or corruption I always told the people every detail even if it was to my detriment. I think many came to trust me.

These virtues were often overshadowed by my increasing clumsiness like the time I fell backward off my chair in the Oval office on national television. I always pretended these fumbles did not happen but everyone knew I was clumsy. Initially my supporters fondly called me Honest Hugh and detractors derisively Clumsy Dangerton, but over time most everyone with a chuckle started calling me just Hugh. My clumsiness brought me notoriety but I like to think I brought a degree of humility and perhaps a little goodness to the world.

Up to now Marxist socialism had been a major cause of human contention. Many past societies, including my America, had failed under its heavy boot and when I took office it appeared world government was going down that unfortunate wood path. It looked like, in a democracy, the biblical admonition that the poor would inherit the earth through socialism was true. My years holding the reins of world power taught me otherwise, I learned that the best brew for a healthy society was capitalist production intelligently managing

Adam Smith's invisible hand creating wealth along with a moderate degree of socialism preventing privation—the best societies have both production and charity. I enjoyed many successes as president of the UNH but the most satisfying was when the Socialistic Pacific States of America, the home of my Oregon, changed its name to the Pacific States of America.

After eight years of power I had had enough. Like pleasure, wealth and prestige power it was just another unsatisfying dead-end street. Deep in thought one day near the end of my last term I had my secretary cancel all my appointments and strolled out of the Brown House and walked through Ellipse Park surrounded by fifty nervous Secret Service agents. I thought about the nature of power and became increasingly cynical. During my time in power I had been surrounded by many ugly, greedy, dishonest and insincere people, courted by sycophants and often vilified for my efforts. I winced when I thought how the few good people in power were treated like my old friend Nagi Naziz who was assassinated. I realized that it did not matter whether I pursued power for prestige or to do good—both were unattainable. Power, like prestige, was just more of the same; I may have done a little good but I could not bring enduring goodness to an evil world. It occurred to me that the dark recesses of human nature cannot be changed through civilization and with this insight I changed.

It was an unsettling seminal time of my life for two reasons. First, I had wasted eighty years of my life outwardly focused trying to be a satisfied pig to no avail. So, I stopped pursuing desires, turned inward and became more introspective. For the rest of my life I sought life-answers in my brain and not out there. The other was I was no longer anonymous. Just about everyone knew about my slowed aging, my wealth from RC Holdings, LLC and my acting career as Hugh Dangerton. The *New York Times* article including photos of me was now part of school history books and throughout the world I was known as Hugh the past president of the United Nations of Humankind. I had become the most recognized human on the planet.

I decided to move on.

CHAPTER 8

Ambiguity

49-52
(2126-2146)

In 2125 I was biologically only 49 years old even though I had lived for 175 years. When my term ended the end of December I called Albert Martin the second and told him to transfer $2 million to my checking account, walked out of the Oval office, went to my apartment, put on some old clothes, got on my bicycle and rode out of Washington. D.C. headed to a small rural town on the West Coast called Walla Walla in the state of Washington. Against all advice I had declined Secret Service protection because I wanted to be free but they had convinced me to wear a GPS warning transmitter around my neck in case of emergency. Later I was glad they did because I would need it.

I was tired of pursuing my passions and wanted something more enduring in life—something concrete. I had enjoyed my years at Oxford and NYU pursuing my PhD in philosophy and had decided that learning could be the answer. So, I rode westward on my bike for an academic place of peace, solitude and contemplation in order to learn and perhaps write.

My plan was to ride the back rural roads of America. It felt good to ride them close to nature with the wind in my face through the old states of Pennsylvania and Ohio, but I quickly realized that things were not the way they used to be in my old America. At the border crossing between the Atlantic States of America and United States of America in Ohio I was detained by a military unit. They were suspicious, took me into an interrogation room and began asking lots of questions. I thought I could be in serious trouble when a Lieutenant entered and said we shoot spies. I immediately took off my wind cap and riding glasses, said I was Hugh Dangerton past president of the United Nations of Humankind, astonished they immediately recognized me, apologized for any inconvenience, gave me my bicycle and a bottle of whiskey and sent me on my way. It felt strange to be arbitrarily suspected and detained, which would never have happened in my America.

I rode on through Indiana and then turned north through Wisconsin and then west across Minnesota. The ride was unlike the last time I had traversed America, in 2061 when I drove Route 66 from Los Angeles to Chicago. There were fewer cars all of which were solar powered. Internal combustion fossil fuel engines were illegal, the central states where the winter temperatures were usually below zero was much warmer with temperatures in the forties and fifties and formerly sparsely populated were now teeming with people who had migrated north to escape the unbearable southern heat.

In small Dupree, South Dakota I damn near died because nobody recognized me. After a long day I rode my bike into town and was immediately accosted by a pot smoking, heavy drinking, scruffy, tattooed, sadistic looking, leather clad motorcycle gang. They yanked me off my bike, pushed me around, punched me and one put his knife to my throat threatening to slit it. I thought it was ironic that after all I had been through in life I was going to die at the hand of some ruffian that apparently tormented and killed people for amusement. I boldly told them who I was, they laughed, I became incensed and pushed my GPS warning transmitter that emitted a very loud siren and all hell broke loose. To the gang's astonishment within five minutes two state police cars screamed in, within fifteen minutes two Cobra helicopter gunships began circling above, within 30 minutes a local detachment of National Guard arrived, within two hours about fifteen black-clad Secret Service agents swarmed the town and shortly thereafter a military unit of the UNH arrived—tanks and all. The threatening biker who had held the knife to my throat in a fit of anger made the fatal mistake of pulling his handgun on one state police officer and immediately died in a fusillade of bullets and the others quickly became compliant. The bikers were arrested, handcuffed and taken off to jail and eventually prosecuted by the UNH Department of Justice. I retrieved my bike, thanked everyone and rode off to the west. The pursuit of power may have been fruitless but it sure came in handy this time.

I rode on through the Badlands of South Dakota, past Mt. Rushmore which had been defaced because the UNH did not like monuments to white men, through Montana and Idaho where I finally arrived in my country the Pacific States of America. My last scrape with destiny was when I got to the state of Washington a few miles out of Walla Walla and ran into a freak snowstorm. I was unprepared when I got hit by high, freezing-snow-filled winds in a whiteout on an icy road on my bike in the middle of nowhere. I fell and lay on the road for a while until a car full of old ladies returning from a bridge game stopped, helped me in their car and drove to Walla Walla. I thanked them for saving my life, got a room at the nearest motel and went into a deep sleep. I had ridden about 4,000 miles in 61 days and needed it.

In the morning I woke up to a new life. Up to now—the last 175 years—it had been fast and dangerous. In hindsight, my time in Walla Walla was the turning point where the last third of it became slower, quieter and peaceful. I had finally found a place to think and ponder away from world's cacophony. Over the years I had heard of this small remarkable liberal arts college, Whitman, isolated in the unpopulated eastern Washington wheat fields and wine country. It was considered one of the best colleges in old America and now the Harvard of the PSA.

I got up, took a shower, dressed and walked to its stately old Memorial building. I asked the receptionist if I could see the Provost for a teaching job to which she loudly exclaimed "MR. PRESIDENT!" With this the room filled with curious administrators and faculty utterly amazed that Hugh Dangerton, the past president of the United Nations of Humankind and famous actor, was standing in their offices. The dazzled president ushered me into her office and asked what she could do for me. I said I wanted to apply for a teaching job in philosophy and described my degrees in philosophy from Oxford and NYU. She was dumbfounded, said sure and hired me.

I settled in, bought a small house near the campus in cash, purchased furniture and appliances and went grocery shopping and started cooking my own meals. I also bought some new clothes because mine were dirty bike touring wear. I rode my bike everywhere, lived simply and enjoyed life in the quiet, peaceful and intimate community of Walla Walla in the intellectual academic atmosphere of Whitman. It felt good to live a simple routine life.

I surveyed my empty house and decided I needed a companion, so I got a dog. I went to the local pound and saw many irritating yipping dogs and almost left until I saw this calm and very handsome golden retriever sitting quietly in a corner of his pen. He caught my attention because he looked pensive like a philosopher, so I took him home. I named him Thad after that awful dishonest broker at CS Corporation because I could tell him what to do. It turned out that Thad had quite a personality. On one hand he was loyal, affectionate and tractable—he was a happy dog. We spent a lot of time together running, hiking and just hanging out. But he was also opinionated and judgmental. If I gave him the wrong dog food or did not let him out when he wanted, he would sit looking at me with a cocked head and growl. If he really got mad he would pee on my shoes when I was not looking. In time, like marriage, we learned the other's foibles and how to live together.

One day after ten years living with Thad, I was amazed to learn a side of him I never knew. We were hiking together in the Blue Mountains outside of Walla Walla when he suddenly started restlessly looking everywhere and then ran off. I did not know what to think so I hiked on thinking he would soon show up until I heard a commotion behind me. I turned and saw a large mountain lion with an open mouth and white wicked fangs bearing down on me: his dinner. I braced myself for his lunge when out of the blue Thad emerged from the bushes and tackled him. There was a furious fight with each viciously biting the other, slashing claws and blood everywhere. I quickly regained my senses, unsheathed my 12-inch Bowie knife, rushed into the fight and stabbed the lion over and over as quick as I could. I felt teeth and claws in my body but kept up the stabbing along with Thad who had him by the throat. Gradually the beast lost strength, whimpered and died limp and bloodied. Thad and I fell back exhausted and seriously bleeding but alive. We managed to get to my car, drove to the nearest hospital and spent hours in their emergency room where the doctors and an on-call emergency veterinarian stitched us up and pumped us full of blood and antibiotics. We survived and the sensational story made national news and we gained some notoriety. After this I looked at Thad with different eyes. He had always been so kind and gentle, but I now knew down deep he was a fierce courageous warrior who would sacrifice his life for me. He had saved my life and gained a special place of respect and honor in my heart. He was a good dog and close companion for the rest of his life.

I settled into a routine of teaching, writing and reading. My philosophy classes became quite popular mostly because I was famous. Students, who had read about me in their history classes, weren't so interested in ancient philosophies like Stoicism, which was my area of specialty, but rather my life. They asked questions about Oxford, my hippie sexual life in San Francisco, my experiences in war, about power and politics and occasionally complained about the coffee I had spilled on their exams because they couldn't read my comments. I became a popular professor with the students even though I got a reputation for clumsiness and smelling like pee.

The history faculty was particularly interested in me because I knew everything about recent history like the American Civil War and formation of the UNH because I had lived some of it and sometimes made it. Over time, my classes became a problem for Whitman's administration because there was so much demand. They began getting requests from reporters, politicians, historians, scientists and businesspeople and later philosophers from all over to attend my classes and had to limit attendance.

The faculty was a potpourri of fascinating learned people of which Bill and Monica in the philosophy department were two favorites. When I first met Bill he said his name was Bill Englesome, I said my major professor at NYU 46 years ago had the same name, he said that was his father and our friendship began seamlessly where the old one left off. It was eerie because he too was stooped and blind in one eye, cranky and funny. Bill was intensely interested in what I knew about his father and asked me many questions. Monica Miller was a young enthusiastic, vulnerable, self-depreciating, lesbian leery of men who said "fuck" a lot in her classes on Arendt and feminism. Once struggling to answer a student question she wrote on the board "I don't know shit." Unbeknownst to me at the time Monica's sexuality was a harbinger of things to come. Psychology professor Robert French was a one-of-a-kind-character from North Carolina where "everyone is related." He had been born in poverty, raised himself by the bootstraps and earned a PhD but still said "winders" for windows and "ci-reen" for siren. The Green was Whitman's favorite pub and I went there often with students and faculty to drink, talk and laugh. It was there that I met Rachel Robertson, who I will describe shortly.

In spite of my dull youth throughout my life I harbored the dream of becoming an author so now I took it up with a vengeance. Between my teaching obligations I fell into a routine of sitting on my bed in the evening drinking Pabst Blue Ribbon beer with the television on mute writing, reviewing it in the morning, researching and thinking about it during the day and then write again in the evening. My first books were uneven but got better with time. Early moderately successful books were *On Humans* about human nature and two on Stoicism titled *Stoicism, Enkrasia and Happiness*, which was my redacted thesis, and *A Reference Guide to Stoicism*. One day I got a call from a producer at Ingram Publishers wanting to sign a contract with me to write my autobiography. Surprised, I said you don't call me, I am supposed to call you and you hang up. He laughed, we signed a contract, I wrote it (some of which is included in this later update of my life), they published and promoted it, it made the *New York Times* bestseller list and I became a famous author. People already knew my life story, but apparently they really liked me describing it.

Sometime around 2140 I went to an American Philosophic Society meeting in Seattle where I got into this intense debate with uptight Christopher Chalmers, a professor of philosophy at Princeton University, on free will and determinism. I don't mean to bore you but historically everyone believed in fate. In the Middle Ages religion conceived of free will to save a benevolent god, and in the early part of the century the idea that it was a false dichotomy arose and the new theory of compatibilism was adopted. Chalmers advocated compatibilism and I argued freedom is based on metaphysics and a deterministic point of view. Chalmers and I carried on a lively, intense and closely watched debate in the Philosophic Society's newsletter, a philosophic doctoral candidate wrote their dissertation on it, which became part of important philosophic literature. I was astounded because I was now not only a famous person and author but now renowned philosopher.

About this time I also took up my goal of learning with a vengeance. I decided the best way to do this was to read of the best books ever written. I researched a number of sources and methodically developed a list of 500 books and started a rigorous daily regimen of reading them. I read every morning for two hours, during the day when I could and in the evening after my writing. I had lots of time because I was only about 50 biologically and aging very slowly. Whitman had an excellent library and over the next 20 years I read everything from Butler's *Erehwon* to William James *The Varieties of Religious Experience*.

What I learned was that the words I read revealed a deeper source of eternal ideas that exist beyond them that had melted into a mass of recurring themes; that words may change but enduring meanings persist. I was thrilled at this discovery because what I had been doing through my reading was realizing Plato's view that true knowledge is like a river of eternal ideas that I came to swim in. He was right. Many of these eternal ideas are scattered throughout this book and in the conclusion.

Between being a professor, writing and reading this was indeed a great learning period of my life but I felt strangely unsatisfied. There always seemed to be something new to teach, creative to write and more to learn which required another book to read.

One of my most unusual and rewarding relationships with a woman began at the Green one night when I met Rachel Robertson. I was having a beer with Bill Englesome, deep in conversation about some esoteric philosophic point when this young braless woman wearing a very open string tank top abruptly sat down in our booth, clearly interested in younger Bill, hugged his arm and began talking in a supplicating manner. I watched with great interest because there was something strangely familiar about her. She said how handsome he was and asked what he was doing that night. Bill was flattered but uneasy because he was married so he smiled, avoided answering her, said see you tomorrow Hugh and left. The young woman was obviously disheartened and sat quietly staring down at the table. I was struck by her angst, reached out and held her hand which she quickly pulled back because she was startled. She looked at me wondering and smiled weakly.

Rachel was a mid-twentyish, plain-looking, poorly dressed and coiffured young woman obviously alone and eager. I said my name was Hugh. She did not recognize me and said she should go. I said I don't know you but I would like to talk to you. Puzzled she said OK. I told her about my slow aging and a few events in my life, which she immediately believed and with this she opened up and began telling me about herself. In a faltering voice she said she was a Townie, had gone to high school in Walla Walla but never graduated.

I told her more about myself, my past family, the pain of lost loves and that I was a professor of philosophy at Whitman and she listened with rapt attention. She opened up further and began describing some of the deep pains in her life including being sexually abused when young and never being asked for a date by the boys in high school because of her looks when all of her girlfriends were. She began sobbing so I took her in my arms in the midst of a raucous bar and just held her crying for a while.

We went to my house where Thad immediately growled at her, she laughed, petted him which he liked and we sat on the sofa, suck-up Thad curled up by her side, and we continued our talk. I poured us some wine and told her more of my life to which she suddenly exclaimed that she had seen me in the newspaper. She became fascinated and asked many questions mostly about my relationships with women. I suddenly realized I was talking with someone much like the young Stella I had known a hundred years ago in Burns, Oregon who had been homely, used and abandoned by the hometown boys and deeply hurt. So, I told her Rachel Stella's story and she again started crying, went stony cold and abruptly left.

Rachel was Stella, an innocent, yeaning and young unattractive woman looking for love and forever being painfully rejected and used by men. Like Stella, Rachel had been ignorantly using her body to get the love she desperately wanted only to be driven to the lowest rungs of society. I was now different and rather than watch from the sidelines I decided to try to do something because I had come to care for this young woman.

A few days later while reading Rachel knocked on my door, I answered and she asked to come in. I said sure and our conversation picked up where it had left off along with suck-up Thad again at her side. She said she had thought a lot about the things I had said and wanted to know more. So, I told her more about Stella, how she had lost her sense of self-respect, her rejection from society and eventual early death. In high emotion Rachel raised her shirt and showed me her breasts, I smiled and to her amazement lowered her shirt and said no. So, my long and unusual Platonic relationship with Rachel began.

We started spending a lot of time together, having dinners, talking about our pasts and discussing her future. We talked about self-respect, dignity, the nature of happiness and desire and education all of which captivated her. It turned out she was quite intelligent and interested in learning. Together we imagined an alternative life for her with an education, career, husband and children which grabbed her imagination. She became one of my best friends—a soul mate.

Over time Rachel changed as a new world was gradually revealed to her. She started wearing less revealing, attractive clean clothes, an elegant braid that accentuated her facial features and less make-up. She grew quieter and more confident. With my encouragement she finished high school with a GED, applied and was accepted to Washington State University, left Walla Walla, graduated from WSU with a degree in biology, went on to veterinarian school at the University of Washington and became a veterinarian. When she left Walla Walla I lost track of her but went back later with OMNI and saw how her life had turned out. She had a successful veterinarian practice, had met a young man, fallen in love, married, started a family and had three children. She looked supremely happy and fulfilled.

Watching Rachel from the future gave me great pleasure and made me think about Rachel's and Stella's lives. One without learning, Stella, had lived in pain and died young while Rachel had learned, lived long and achieved happiness. I thought it may be true that knowledge is empty because there is always something new to learn but practically it can bring a better life like it did for Rachel.

While on OMNI, I also decided to visit my old companion Thad one last time. He was old with cancer but as handsome and loyal as ever. I watched him in pain during his last few days, relived my grief when I took him to the veterinarian to be euthanized, watched the doctor inject a syringe filled with a sinister orange liquid into his body and see him quickly fade. I had forgotten that he growled at me just before he died. I relived the sadness of the loss of an old friend. I still miss him.

About this time, Stella's and Rachel's relations with men, Monica's lesbianism, Whitman College president's same-sex marriage, my male friends' strange longings for a traditional woman along with my own relationships with women made me more aware of the human sexual and reproductive revolution that had been silently evolving over the last two hundred years.

For thousands of years women's reproductive powers had been controlled by religion or the state. They married for life, procreated children and raised them in families but with the advent of democracy in the late eighteenth century, their right to vote and a pill to prevent pregnancy in the twentieth century they began controlling their own sexuality and reproductive ability. It began with a feminist movement and legal abortion and was quickly followed by the LBGT movement or lesbian, bisexual, gay or transsexual rights and same-sex marriage.

Sexual liberation was given a strange twist by science when it discovered how to manufacture artificial ova and semen which gave men and women the ability to reproduce individually. It had come a long way since my designer baby beginnings. Huge banks of gametes were created and around 2140, human reproduction was taken out of God's hands and gender became irrelevant. A trend began to humans of the same gender or unisex. The consequences were ominous. The sole reason for sexuality became pleasure and the act became like shaking hands. It was no longer special. It became an orgy of exchanging fluids like San Francisco and New York now times twenty. The institution of marriage faded, the abortion issue evaporated, families faded into history and the state started raising the children. As male and female traits faded a new kind of blended person began to emerge. It was a strange hybrid that melded strength, weakness, aggressiveness and meekness into a bland kind of sameness. Increasingly absent were any individuality, uniqueness and conflict was replaced by an uninteresting uniform monotonous character. This new emerging race of humans called Unities, which was benign and bereft of vitality, began reproducing themselves. It turned out that their progenies were weak, their survival instinct attenuated, sometimes died early and often impotent. Isolated communities of Unities started but became extinct over time.

The biggest problem that arose was moral. Because any individual could reproduce, reproduction became chaotic with overpopulation in some places, very strange people in others and Unities everywhere. The burning issue of who is to be born and who is to die emerged, which caused the United Nations of Humankind to intervene. With this the human race began eugenics and the government started deciding what constitutes the best kind of human being, which quickly became political and the contest became who gets to design humanity. At the time I was confused and did not know how this would all work out. I did know that Unities produced poor offspring recalling ancient Roman author Juvenal's advice that it is best to stay in gender, but I was left with the question whether it is better to reproduce through chance or design. I did not know how human sexuality would work out until much later.

At age 52 biologically and 200 chronologically after many wonderful years in Walla Walla I was disappointed. I had spent much of my early life pursuing pleasure as a satisfied pig and after twenty years learning as a dissatisfied Socrates and I still did not know which was better. On one hand the early passions I had pursued had brought excitement and happiness but also a more-of-the-same ennui. It was like being Stella and ending up nowhere. On the other hand pursuing learning had also brought excitement, happiness and a better life much like Rachel's experience. But as I learned more, I found there was always more to learn because knowledge only seemed to bring ambiguity. The more I learned the less I knew. There was always another book to read in order to understand and when I read the ostensible answer the problem the persisted.

Famous ancient nineteenth-century English philosopher David Hume, who I had studied at Oxford, wrote that reason is and ought to be the slave of the passions. It occurred to me everything I had wanted in life required desire to pursue all of which ironically had extinguished my desire to pursue them. After my early pursuits of sensual pleasure, money, celebrity and power I had lost my interest in them. And now after years of learning I had lost that desire as well. My confusion was because desire itself seemed to go nowhere, so I decided to try something deeper, perhaps more profound beyond desire. Faith-based spirituality seemed the answer so I decided to pursue it.

I also had been getting uncomfortably hot in Walla Walla. Being in a temperate zone historically its summers had been hot, around 76 degrees Fahrenheit, and cold in the winter, usually around 35 degrees. Now the summers were uncomfortably hot at around 90 and often 100 degrees and winters mild, usually around 50 degrees. So, I told the administration I was leaving, sold my house, bought a vintage 2120 solar-powered car, said goodbye to colleagues, friends and students and headed out of town after my last class.

CHAPTER 9

The Other Side

53-58
(2147-2190)

It felt like old times, being on the road again in my vintage solar-electric car heading out to some unknown destination with adventure in the air. In the 1970s I had visited Lhasa, Tibet, which left a lifelong impression on me. I recalled its mystical spiritual Buddhist aura and felt drawn to it. However, I wanted to see the widely reported southern heat firsthand so I drove south on old Highway 395 through Oregon, into the former Socialistic Pacific States of America where I hit intact but decaying Interstate 5 at Red Bluff and continued south.

Even though I was only 53 years old biologically I had lived 200 years and was beginning to feel the slow effects of aging. My life began getting slower, quieter and peaceful. My body was becoming weaker, my mind duller and I began getting more ailments which took longer to recover from. It also seemed like the wheels were coming off the world. The radioactive fallout from earlier nuclear wars that had killed some areas of the world were not abating and widespread illness was increasing due to different virulent strains of disease along with bacteria that were increasingly resistant to antibiotics. But the most fearsome was the earth's temperature, which had been increasing unabated over the last 150 years. It had made many areas, mostly near the equator, uninhabitable. Hawaii, for example, had become too hot to live in.

Unbeknownst to me at the time I still had another 8 biologic and 100 chronological years left to live and felt up to it. I took my problems in stride and made the most of whatever I had left in life. In hindsight, my old adventurous, insouciant and glad-to-be-alive character asserted itself. I knew then there would be less action and excitement but looked forward to a deeper, more interesting and contemplative life in spiritual Tibet.

Traveling south on I-5 the first thing I noticed was the decreasing traffic and heat. I was surprised that the border crossing into the SPSA had been abandoned which seemed eerily strange. The landscape gradually changed from green to brown to barren and finally gray desert in some areas which were insufferably hot. I quickly discovered there was little government, no police and lawlessness. Around Sacramento I ran into a roadblock of wrecked cars with many starving emaciated-looking bandits totally unlike the gangs on Springwater Corridor 137 years earlier or the ruthless bikers I had encountered in Dupree, South Dakota 21 years ago. They wanted anything I had in order to survive. From behind their barricade they shot at me and threw rocks. I no longer had my UNH GPS warning transmitter because there was no longer a UNH, so I reached into my satchel and pulled out a hand grenade.

As a souvenir from the past I had saved one grenade from my old M4 Carbine Commando grenade launcher that I had bought in Los Angeles and used to protect myself from Los Angeles rioters and thwart pirates off the coast of Indonesia. It had been in storage when I was in the Grey house and on my mantle in my Walla Walla house. It was very old and I did not know if it would work but I pulled the pin, threw it at them, it blew up, they scattered like lemmings and I continued my journey south.

Around Bakersfield it got very hot. It was an unbearable heat I had never experienced—it was like being in an oven. I had read that death is almost certain for humans at 111 degrees but that some had been known to survive in 115-degree heat. When cooked, people usually go into continuous convulsions, then shock and finally cardio-respiratory collapse and death. I was sweating, mildly delirious and feeling involuntary muscle contractions when I pulled into this old abandoned gas station and saw an ancient thermometer that said 116 degrees and immediately decided to turn around and head north as fast as I could.

In hindsight I now realize how lucky I was to have lived. If I had stayed in that heat for another 30 minutes, I would have cooked to death. Racing north I was horrified by the thought that this northward advance of heat due to global warming would someday make earth uninhabitable, although at the time I was unaware that it would be impeded by cold air coming down from the melting North Pole. While traveling north it gradually cooled and I realized for the first time that humanity's nest is going away. The dead, lifeless and extreme heat, now called the KHZ or Killing Heat Zone, would continue to advance, which I will describe later. At Sacramento I was confronted by the same bandit roadblock but this time they recognized me and scattered like lemmings to avoid another grenade. I continued north, drove through Portland to SeaTac airport near Seattle, said goodbye to my vintage car, went into the terminal and bought a one-way ticket on Han Airways to Lhasa and took off into the night for the other side of the globe and my new spiritual life.

I flew to Beijing and Szechwan and over the Himalayas to Lhasa, landed at their airport that I had forgotten was an hour from the city, exited the plane and suddenly felt a rush of welcome cold air. Tibet's 12,000 ft. altitude was refreshingly different than southern California's insufferable heat. I took a bus through the grand and stark Yarlung valley along the Yarlung River to Lhasa, checked in to the still oddly fashionable Holiday Inn, immediately got altitude sickness, drank a beer in the bar and went to bed.

I got up early in the morning feeling great and, like I had 167 years earlier, took a long walk through cool downtown Lhasa. I wandered through Barkor Square, the Peoples Park and around the Portola Palace and again smelled the incense and watched Tibetans spinning their prayer wheels and singing mantras. Little had changed—it was still the same old, magical, ineffable and ancient

Buddhist culture. I was comforted by the thought that it would have been the same had I been there 1,000 years earlier. The last time I visited Lhasa there was Chinese military everywhere but they were now gone and the people looked happier because, like my old America, communist China had Balkanized years earlier and left Tibet. This made me proud because it was partly due to my policy as president of the UNH to both assimilate countries but allow them to retain their individual culture, which had accelerated China's collapse and abandonment of Lhasa. It had also allowed the Dali Lama to return home. It seemed to me that they had regained their old pride and dignity as a people. Perhaps above all I felt free because nobody recognized me.

So, after my walk I went to the prestigious Johkang Monastery to apply to become a monk, not knowing they do not apply but rather chosen. The puzzled monks took me to see the enigmatic head priest Bhikkhu Bodhi who did not know who I was but was curious why a strange tall white man wanted to talk with him. I said I was a Stoic philosopher who wanted to know more about Buddhist spiritualism, which caught his interest because he knew they were similar and after a few questions he accepted me into their brotherhood and my spiritual journey began.

My life abruptly became slower, sedentary and contemplative. All my worldly possession were taken, including any money on me. I was given a simple robe to wear and shown a small room with a bed. I started taking daily classes, studied the Buddhist bible called the Tripitaka and the ancient Indian language Pali, learned mantras, prayed daily and often sat on the roof of the monastery with Bodhi drinking tea and talking. We talked about philosophy, religion and spirituality and over time became great friends.

Gradually our conversations became deeper and more personal. Bodhi was born into a traditional family but was chosen when very young to become a Buddhist priest, which was a great honor. He left home when young, was raised in the monastery and at sixteen was required to spend a year on a pilgrimage begging. I told him about my slowed aging, my ancient family and some of my adventures, which fascinated him. I avoided mentioning my acting and political careers because I wanted a normal relationship. Bodhi told me that Buddhist priests are forbidden to touch women, have sex or marry because celibacy is needed to reach enlightenment. He said the only way for a woman to give him food was by putting it in a bowl and leaving. He said that it was during his pilgrimage he fell in love with a woman, married her and had children. He said it was a scandal but the senior priests decided to look the other way, but he would never rise in the church hierarchy. He said he loved his wife and children and cheerfully had no regrets.

Many of our conversations were on Buddhism. He taught me the four noble truths, which were existence is suffering, the cause of suffering is craving and attachment, there is a path to the cessation of suffering and that path is nirvana or a transcendent state bereft of desire or sense of self in which one is released from the cycle of death and rebirth. I taught him much Western philosophy from Plato and Stoicism to Nietzsche. We particularly enjoyed comparing Buddhism and Stoicism and wondering if it was Alexander the Great who transmitted it to Greek culture in 300 BCE. I have often gone back in OMNI to relive these precious conversations and the alternate world of spiritualism I was living with my old friend Bodhi.

One day out of the blue Bodhi and I were asked to go to the Portola Palace because the Dali Lama wanted to see us. I was thrilled and Bodhi was worried because he thought he had done something wrong. The Palace had not changed a bit—it was still a dark, dank musty smelling magical dungeon-like place with red-robed Buddhists in every nook and cranny singing mantras over butter lamps. We were ushered in to the Lama's private bedroom. I tripped over the door sill, accidently knocking over a butter lamp that caught a monk's robe on fire. He screamed, tore it off and, naked, pounded it trying to put it out while I walked over amongst the smoke as if nothing happened and introduced myself. Obviously amused, the Dali Lama said, "Hi Hugh, I've heard a lot about you" and Bodhi was stunned the Dali Lama knew me.

It turned out he knew everything about me. He thanked me for helping his brother monks escape certain death from the Chinese 170 years ago and for freeing his country from Chinese occupation as the

United Nations of Humankind President which also allowed him to return home. He said I know you are the richest man in the world, that you are a celebrated actor and have scholastic learning but what we admire the most is your longevity. We Buddhists revere old people because they are wise and, at 200 years, you are by far the oldest of us all. We are honored to have you with us. Poor Bodhi now was speechless.

I said it is me who is honored to be with you and with this the Dali Lama and I began one of the most wide-ranging, deep, multi-layered interesting conversations of my life. It was like after thousands of years of evolving different ways of thinking, East and West finally sat down to compare notes. We disagreed a lot. He said humans are collectivistic and cited Confucius I said they are individuals and quoted Thomas Jefferson. He said the mind and body are separate and I described Descartes' dualism and its problems. He claimed humans are non-violent and I said psychologist Freud believed they are violent because civilization represses their instincts. He said there is an afterlife and I said yes, it is called dirt and he laughed. He believed in innate knowledge and I said Plato did also but nurture has much influence and cited Aristotle, who emphasized habit. He said nothing is permanent and change is always possible and I described Plato's forms. He said all is determined and I said compatabilism says otherwise. He said we must have empathy for others and I in spirit agreed but conditioned it with Thomas Malthus' truism that the more need you feed the more you get and that feeding need does not address causes, only consequences. He said he disdained politics and I agreed but said it being other means than war is a better way.

We spent a lot of time discussing faith and reason. He said faith is essential to achieve nirvana and I said Erasmus thought being deceived by faith makes us happy but we discarded that idea long ago. I said faith is an assumption whose greatest enemy, according to spiritualist Reinhold Niebuhr, is doubt. I also said only reasons eventually achieve truth which irritated him. He said wisdom brings enlightenment and not rationality and that spirituality and faith's greatest enemy is rationality and the intellect. I said rationality brings truth and cited Cicero, who wrote it is what distinguishes us from the beasts. I also mentioned Western civilization's greatest achievements like science and pointed out that the East's spirituality is just more of the same. I did condition this point with Hume's reason is the slave of the passions but claimed reason can influence our passions and thus how to act.

We also agreed a lot. We agreed virtue is supreme and above externals, that one must improve themselves before others and that it is best to live a simple life. He said there is no god only Siddhartha Gautama's nirvana and I agreed citing Spinoza's *Ethics* and pantheism. We agreed suffering comes from craving and attachment to externals and the solution was to become detached and the need to subdue passion. I said Cicero wrote that the turbulent tossing of soul whipped by passion leaves no room for the happy life. We agreed most people's minds are more taken with appearances than reality and I mentioned Erasmus, and that happiness comes from within and achieving a tranquil mind.

After our marathon talk, we took a break, relaxed and drank some potent qingke Tibetan beer, got a little buzzed and our conversation became more intimate. We concluded that even though our cultures had evolved in different ways we had always been after the same objective—human happiness. After a while he smiled and said Hugh, you are a wise and good person but a lousy Buddhist monk and I smiled and said Lama you are also a wise and good person but would make a poor scientist and we both laughed. I got up, said goodbye, knocked over a butter lamp that caught the rug on fire and left.

Because we had talked all night, it was morning when an uncharacteristically quiet Bodhi and I walked through Lhasa back to the monastery. Obviously agitated, he blurted you should have told me who you are—I feel like a fool! I smiled at him and said if I had you would not have become the friend you are. He smiled back thoughtfully and we walked on in silence.

The conversation with the Dali Lama left me with much to think about. I began thinking spirituality may not be for me and that I might leave. I wondered if I leave, where will I go and what will I do? But, I decided to give spiritualism one more try in my pilgrimage.

So, later I left the monastery and went on my year-long required neophyte monk pilgrimage. It was the first time in my life having no money, extra clothes or food, which made it kind of an exciting adventure. I hiked the Himalayan highlands, ate bits of food people left out for me and slept in the open, usually shivering in my thin robe. I loved the irony of the richest man in the world being penniless and begging for food. At one time I was heartily welcomed at the Drepung Monastery, given food and a place to sleep.

Near Zhegu, I serendipitously came across a small commune of people happily laughing and dancing during their monthly festival of life celebration. They immediately welcomed me because I was a Buddhist monk and offered me some food. I learned it was an American expatriate spiritual commune and was particularly glad nobody recognized me. My first impressions soon gave way to curiosity as I noticed some evasive and furtive eyes, I began feeling something was wrong.

Shortly their spiritual leader emerged from his hut and heartily greeted me as a fellow spiritualist. He was tall, dark and quite handsome, with piercing black eyes. He said his name was Jim Black but everyone called him Jimmy and welcomed me to his cult. We talked for a while and I was impressed with his strong charismatic, magnetic and friendly personality. He talked about America, spiritualism, LSD, women and a place called the other side and asked about me. I said I was a simple Buddhist neophyte monk on my pilgrimage and he smiled. I had known many people in my life and had become a pretty good judge of character and my intuition told me to be careful around this person. He asked me to stay for a while and I said sure, not wanting to appear rude.

I learned more than I wanted about this cult over the next few weeks. Jim was a famous discredited American college professor due to his advocacy of hallucinogenic drugs—mostly mind-altering LSD. I went to a few of his sermons and he would stress the importance of getting to the other side, or beyond the door as he called it, and claim the way was through LSD. He would say that the mind is constantly dulled by everyday information and LSD sharpens the blade. Over time, I noticed that he could only describe the world beyond the door in metaphors and parables and never explicitly.

As a person seeking spirituality I became increasingly dismayed by the cult. They appeared to be dissatisfied and restless young people who had been afflicted by problems they could not handle, people without motivation and ambition who disdained bourgeoisie society and who wallow in self-pity. They, for example, would jejunely say whatever was needed would be provided. They increasingly looked like easily duped, gullible and credulous non-conformists and maladjusted failures. It looked to me that they were using psychedelic drugs to escape a world they could not cope with. I began to wonder if these are the kinds of people naturally attracted to spiritualism.

To make matters worse, I discovered that promiscuity was ubiquitous. Everybody constantly had sex with everybody else—it was like San Francisco times 100. They would get high and then spend hours in rapturous orgasm. One day I met Ginger, an innocent, bubbly, absent-minded early-twentyish commune woman in the bloom of her feminine beauty. We struck up a friendly conversation and talked about her life. I asked if she had a family back home and she hesitated, said yes but had run away and changed the subject. I asked why she ran away and she again hesitated, said because her parents had grounded her and changed the subject. I asked her why her parents had grounded her and she said because she was skipping high school and again changed the subject. I had obviously touched a sensitive nerve but intuited she had something to get out so I asked her if her parents were good to her? Her face went sad and after a long pause she said in a low quiet voice yes—they wanted me to go to college. I asked her if she wanted to go to college, there was another long pause, she said yes and then started quietly sobbing. Instinctively I put my arms around little Ginger and held her close for a long time. When she had calmed down, somber and red-eyed, she said in a quavering voice I love my parents and desperately want to go home. I asked her why she had not gone home and she said because she had met a man who introduced her to drugs, made her have sex with his friends, got pregnant and had a baby that she gave away. She said she did not think her parents would want her back. Then she went quiet and again wept for a while and finally said I wish I could live my life over. Then excitedly she said but my new father Jimmy saved me and I am now free! Silently I looked at her and thought what a tragic story for a pretty young woman. I thought how hopeless, drugged, strung-out and brainwashed this poor young capricious girl was. Unlike Stella or Rachel, she had lost all will or conviction, her brain appeared fried and dismayed I realized there was nothing I could do to help her. After our conversation I noticed that she was widely used sexually in the cult, spent a lot of time in Jim's hut and mysteriously disappeared one day. I asked some members what had happened to her and only got blank stares and silence.

After a couple of weeks I began feeling something was terribly wrong. The once-friendly members had become more cool and suspicious and I felt watched. I had overheard some of them talking about earlier devotees who had been "sent on" and wondered where that was and if Ginger had been one of them. I decided something sinister was going on and to find out what it was. The obvious suspect was Jim Black, so I began finding out more about him. I snuck into his office one night, searched some files and then saw a large black pot with some brew in it with two bottles of strychnine and sodium cyanide poison beside it, wondered what they were for and slipped out the back door.

The next day I warily went to their monthly festival of life celebration and watched Jim bring out the pot of brew proclaiming it was an enchanted psychedelic drink that would take them to the other side and encouraged all to imbibe. I put two and two together, unthinking ran to the pot, took some brew and poured it into one of the dogs' dishes which one quickly drank. I looked at the members and screamed Jim's brew is poison, do not drink it! Jim immediately called me Satan and a traitor which inflamed the crowd who started surrounding me with drawn knives. I thought good god, I almost died 64 years ago when a crazy motorcycle gang member almost slit my throat and now I am going to be killed by a bunch of deranged druggies. Suddenly the dog yelped, went into convulsions and died, the stunned members looked at me and then Jim. He ran, but they caught him and brutally stabbed him to death.

It turned out Jim had been poisoning cult members, including poor Ginger, with a brew of poison and LSD, believing it would send them to the other side, which turned out to be death. The members thanked me and asked if I would stay but I had had enough. Disillusioned, I left, quit my pilgrimage early and went back to the monastery.

When I got back to Lhasa, I was surprised to see it crowded with thousands of new people. I went to the monastery and found Bodhi and asked him what was going on. Worried, he said people of the lowlands had been flocking to Lhasa due to the heat. I learned many people had been dying from heat at lower altitudes so they were escaping to the cool cocoon high in the Himalayan Mountains. I shuddered because I had experienced killing heat 43 years earlier in California. I remembered the tear-gas-like pockets of polluted hot air, my gasping lungs, convulsions and the unbearable heat. I remembered what it is like to be cooked. I was shaken from my spiritual escape by the ominous specter of global warming and killing zone heat.

I learned that the earth's average temperature had gone up 9 degrees, to a worldwide average of 67 degrees, that whole areas had become uninhabitable and there had been massive migration. There was some good news that the advance of the heat had slowed but most believed it was only a matter of time before it resumed. I had thought long ago that the earth was dying and could not help thinking about how foolish humankind is.

For thousands of years, humans' population was small because nature kept it that way with disease and famine. Then suddenly around 1700, only a few hundred years ago, human reason emerged, science began and humans began thwarting nature. It seemed good at the time with miracle medicines, agricultural innovation and faster travel with the internal combustion engine. Then came the industrial revolution in the early 1800s that provided science's innovations to all. But it took only 300 years to see the consequences of humans' hegemony over nature. Massive overpopulation, polluted atmosphere and now global warming were the ominous consequences. Our reason and science had upset the delicate balance of nature and now nature was unleashing the forces that had prevented our planet from being fried by the sun. I thought one cannot blame humans for using reason to improve their instinct to survive, but I also thought how foolish we had been to allow our appetites to forever want more rather that intelligently live within nature's patterns.

The Dali Lama had been right; I was a lousy Buddhist. I had become disillusioned and skeptical. The cult had turned me off. The followers were shallow people escaping the real world seeking another world that does not exist through drugs, sometimes acting like unthinking robots that can follow evil leaders like Jim who killed Ginger. I knew there were other more profound forms of spiritualism like Buddhism that offer a way to think, live and be happy. They are salubrious forms of spirituality that help some cope with reality and their daemons. But I was happy and had no daemons so spirituality seemed silly and pointless—I thought there were better things to do than wander around alone half naked begging for food. I decided, unlike spirituality, reason actually accomplishes something. Spirituality was just make-believe, false wisdom and, like the other human desires, more of the same. Philosophy had always championed reason so I decided to move on to it.

I did not stay long at the monastery. I collected my old clothes and possessions, said goodbye to Bodhi and caught the first bus to Lhasa's airport. The airport terminal was hectic, filled with terrified-looking people escaping the heat. I boarded an Icelandic Airlines flight to Anchorage, Alaska because I had learned that RC Holdings, LLC had relocated there and took off for my new life as a philosopher.

CHAPTER 10

Reason

59-60
(2191-2220)

We landed late in the evening. I grabbed my pack and hailed a ride to downtown Anchorage. The cabbie said $25, I pulled out my old wallet and found about $250 of rumpled old American dollars and luckily discovered they were still accepted. I said the historic Anchorage Hotel but was told rooms were $800 a night, so he dropped me off at a cheap motel at $200. I checked in and went to bed with $25 to my name.

Like in Walla Walla 65 years earlier, I woke up feeling optimistic and eager to tackle my new life. I walked downtown to RC Holdings, LLC's offices which were now a two-story walk-up wood frame building. I thought wow, this is a far cry from the top floors of the Freedom Tower in New York. When I went in everyone was wearing t-shirts and jeans including the managing director who happened to be standing in the hall. I looked at him, said I was Reggie Calhoun and he said coolly his name was Albert Martin the third and he was tired of being pestered. It was déjà vu, I laughed, put my hand on his shoulder and described starting the company in the late 1900s, the legal battle to regain ownership in 2070, hiring his grandfather who had just graduated from Harvard in 2080, their Policies and Procedures manual that I had written and said he looked just like his dad.

Now wide-eyed and reverential, he said hello Mr. Calhoun, I have heard a lot about you. He said New York had got to hot so they moved the company to Anchorage, now the financial center of the world, and that the fund's assets had dwindled to $100 million because most assets had burned up. I said thanks, please get me a checking account and transfer $5 million into it. As an afterthought, I asked if he knew anything about my family. He said they had tried to stay in touch with my descendants in the event I died but my last known descendant, probably from the fourth or fifth generation, had died many years ago. I thanked him and left. Walking back to the motel I felt quite alone in the world. I was biologically 58 years old, chronologically about 240 years, all my descendants were gone and my aging had slowed even more. I felt sad and bent but not deterred. At the motel I got my pack, went to the airport and took the first flight to Oxford, England.

It had been 220 years since I graduated from Oxford, the oldest university in the English-speaking world, at age 20. Academically I had come a long way since then, having earned a PhD in philosophy at NYU and being a professor of philosophy at Whitman. Excitedly, I went directly from the airport to the Oxford visitor center and asked the young receptionist if I could see when she abruptly said Mr. Calhoun we were expecting you and took me across campus to The Clarendon administrative building and into the Vice Chancellor's office. The Vice Chancellor said they had received a call from an assistant to the Dali Lama, who I assumed was Bodhi, saying I was coming. He then said since you graduated from Oxford we have followed your career with interest and then without hesitation we would like to give you an honorary PhD and Don emeritus position so you can continue your scholarship studies here. I thought after years as a poor monk this is incredible, said I would be honored, thanked him and it is good to be back. The Vice Chancellor said it is good to have you back. With that, my long life met its natural denouement.

John L. Bowman

My Shakespearian mask disappeared and my final years at Oxford began.

With $5 million in the bank I found a nice apartment near campus, spent time walking the campus reminiscing about old times, thought about my long-dead roommate Charlie Marlboro and his sister Madeline and spent time at the local pubs talking with the young students. I loved to think about all the famous philosophers who had walked Oxford's halls like Duns Scotus, William of Ockham, Thomas Hobbes, John Locke and Jeremy Bentham—they made me feel at home.

Never far from my mind during this time was global warming because I had experienced it firsthand in California. Oxford was still cool and damp but it was also noticeably warmer. Earth's latitude lines are from 0 at the equator to 90 degrees at the poles. Los Angeles, where I first began feeling the heat 100 years ago, is 34 degrees and now uninhabitable. The heat had stopped advancing north at 40 degrees in mid-California and my hometown of Portland at 45 degrees was still habitable; however, RC Holdings had moved out of New York which is also at 45 degrees, to Anchorage at 60 degrees. The only reason I had been able to stay in Lhasa at 30 degrees was because of its altitude. This is why Oxford at 52 degrees, 7 degrees north of Portland, along with the westerly cool winds off the Atlantic Ocean, had stayed so generally cool. But I knew it was only a matter of time.

My plan was to write books on some of my favorite ancient philosophers like Epictetus, Seneca and Epicures along with a few later ones like Locke, Hume and Arendt and quickly fell into the habit researching during the day, going to a local pub to have dinner and review the material and writing in the evening drinking Pabst Blue Ribbon beer. It was at the White Horse Pub one night when this older, plain but appealing looking fiftyish woman said hi, my name is Mary Magdalene. Smiling, I said you have an unusual name, to which she grimaced in a way that revealed she had endured a lifetime of teasing about it. I said I liked it, quickly changed the subject and asked her to join me.

Mary was a sociology professor at Oxford who had spent her life studying the role of women in society. She was an intelligent, highly educated woman with a PhD who had taught feminist and sociology classes for decades. We talked easily about Tong's classic *Feminist Thought* and the unisex movement. She then said she knew about my life, had wanted to meet me and started asking questions like how does it feel to be 250 years old, what was the UNH like and what kind of person is the Dali Lama.

She then asked why I was at Oxford, what I thought about people and world affairs. I pondered for a bit then told her that I was pursuing philosophy at Oxford because I thought reason might solve some of humans' problems, but it had been a mixed blessing. On one hand reason brought revolutionary advances in science, technology and computers, but on the other it has been a dangerous revolution, not knowing where it is going like an unguided ballistic missile that has caused innumerable problems. It brought us nuclear weapons that killed millions, bioengineering that gave us longer lives but also overpopulation that has outstripped our planet's resources, artificial intelligence and rebellious human-like computers that now demand the right to electricity, social media that isolates us causing more suicides and faster non-human time that has detached us from the rhythms of nature. But the worst is global warming that is destroying our planet and then described my close-to-death experience with heat in California. Mary listened intently.

She then quietly asked about Ella and if she had been happy. I said yes, quite happy with her home and children. Then she looked at me pensively and again went quiet. After a long silence she became more animated and personal. She said when she was young she had been an ardent feminist who hated patriarchy. She said a man had loved her and asked her to marry but she turned him down because she preferred her career. She then said she often wondered how her life might have been different if she had married.

With this Mary launched into thoughtful views on women and society. She said feminism had been both good and bad—women had gained a lot but also lost much. She had a rewarding career but the institution of marriage had faded, children were raised in sterile institutions, many women mourned childlessness, men had come to treat women more combatively and harsh as competitors, women had lost their former position of honor and the special bond between the sexes had faded. Rhetorically she asked if, like a pendulum, feminism had gone too far. Then, she looked at me and in a whisper said she wished she had been Ella.

We then discussed how intense passions often interfere with relationships between the sexes when young, how nice it is to be older and free of them and the importance of friendship. With this Mary and I became close Platonic friends and spent a lot of time together as old-age companions at Oxford.

Because of the advances in science and technology I decided one day that I wanted to take some classes in computer science. I quickly found myself in a new world. I studied software design, algorithms, applications, learned new languages such as procedural and functional programming, scripting, C++ and the ancient Pascal language. It was an alternate, artificial cyberspace unreal world of x's, o's and numbers. I struggled to learn this computer knowledge and decided to get a tutor. In hindsight, fate took me to Allan Freedenhoff who was the perfect embodiment of a nerd. Allan was a tall, thin and gangly, wore white short-sleeve shirts with a pocket protector for his pens, spoke with a lisp and was clumsier than me. He had a PhD in computer science from MIT and was considered a brilliant mathematician who always gets the wrong answer.

Allan was a good tutor and over time we became friends. I learned that he was a sensitive, caring and humble outcast nerd. He was also quite interested in me and asked many questions about my past. Mary and I started having dinners with him and our conversations, that usually triangulated sociology, computer science and philosophy, created some unusual interdisciplinary insights. Allan was excitable and would sometimes get carried away and say something incomprehensible like BASIC and C along with COBOL upset his java calculations today so he used FORTRAN and Ada to launch his C#, BASIC cHTM and AspecC++. Mary and I would just look at each other puzzled and implore Allan to speak English and make sense! In time Mary and I grew quite fond of him.

During one tutorial Allan started talking about a computer program he had worked on that could see the past but quit the effort because he could not get it to work. This caught my interest but for now I had to deal with a contentious issue in the philosophy department.

I met many bright philosophers at Oxford. One in particular was Bill Collins who was a middle-aged, mild-mannered Hume scholar who carried a small dog everywhere. He was so kind and gentle with it at first I thought him rather effeminate, but over time we had many intense philosophic conversations, got to know each other and became friends. He was to surprise me greatly at the next faculty meeting.

Philosophy departments are notoriously contentious and Oxford's was particularly so with many egoistic professors protecting their intellectual positions. At one regular meeting of the department I unwittingly started an intense debate that shook the ivy walls to their foundation and started a political firestorm.

I said at a faculty meeting that I thought global warming was humanity's greatest threat and wondered why humans had not used their reason to prevent it. In the back of my mind was David Hume, whom I had studied at NYU and Whitman, who had famously written that reason is the servant of the passions, as well as my debate with the Dali Lama on reason and faith. I said I had come to Oxford to find truth which I thought could be achieved through reason but now was not so sure because humans could not use it to solve global warming. Finally, I said almost in passing that it looks to me now that reason is impotent, it is passion that caused the problem, and all hell broke loose.

Epicurean scholar Professor Edward Seger coldly said how dare you accuse passion of such a crime, it is the source of all human happiness; Professor Eve Courtney, a Hume scholar, jumped to her feet and said no, it is reason that has improved humans' lives in spite of passion's influence; then Professor Kevin Still, a Platonist, advanced into Professor Courtney's face and red-faced said you rational people leave no room for metaphysics and forms, which sent Professor Tom Spelain, a Descartes rationalist philosopher, ballistic. He also jumped to his feet and exclaimed your metaphysics are the problem, always looking for something that does not exist, to which Scholastic Professor Bill Berstein yelled your reason only undermines faith which is the only source of truth and it is the hubris of human reason that is the culprit! Then to my astonishment gentile Professor Bill Collins excitedly jumped up and yelled his father was right, I was a fool and threw his water glass at me! I learned later that his mother's maiden name was Engleson and he was the grandson of the Bill Engleson I knew 120 years ago at NYU and son of the Bill Engleson I knew 60 years ago at Whitman. Instinctively I went to talk with him but tripped and fell on him which he thought was an attack, he threw a punch at me, missed and hit Professor Jim Green behind me in the jaw and with that an academic brawl ensued. Staid philosophy professors who are usually calm, controlled, decorous and erudite began pushing, shoving and fist fighting! Professor Bill Evert sucker-punched Professor Dave Wilder, Professor Eve Courtney kicked Professor Kevin Still in the groin and Professor Bill Berstein had a choke hold on Professor Edward Seger! Finally the astonished campus police came and broke it up but the next day a local newspaper ran a story about how the Oxford philosophy department had gotten into a brawl over whether it was reason or passion that had caused global warming.

Their story hit the newswire and within days a contentious worldwide political debate ensued because suffering people wanted a villain for causing global warming. Some said reason had caused it and others passion. Ancient American philosopher William James once wrote that there are two kinds of people, hard-hearted and tender-hearted. In hindsight I think the former are reason-oriented and the later passion-oriented, that it has always been a natural division within humans and that the issue of global warming was just the impetus for their eternal dispute.

As a result of this, I became even more disillusioned with reason. I thought how reason could possibly prevail over passion when ostensibly rational philosophers easily become emotionally driven children. The issue seemed hopeless to me.

At my next tutorial with Allan we again talked about time travel. Animated he started talking about the problems he encountered with his computer program and rambled on about Einstein's field equations, Quantum Theory, curves, the time loop and wormholes, none of which I understood. Stupidly I said Allan why not just create a computer program that mimics the present and then back it up, or run it backwards like a movie reel? It seems to me you don't need to go to the past physically but only be able to watch it. Allan thought for a minute, got really excited and yelled yes—I got it! He ran back to his laboratory and went into feverish work for days and nights working on his new computer time program.

I remember it vividly. It was May 25, 2210 and Mary was at my house when Allan called and said get over here now, I did it! We ran across the campus to his laboratory, he took us into a small room and started punching on the keyboard. Suddenly the room was filled with a mirror of us now as a hologram, Allan said watch this and punched some more keys and we saw ourselves so lifelike a few minutes ago running across campus! Then he said watch this, punched a few more keys and then utterly astonished we watched the Allied D-day invasion of Normandy in ancient World War Two in 1944. It was so lifelike, in color, we could hear all the sounds and see the bullets flying by and the soldiers fighting. We were astonished. For the first time in history, Allan Freedenhoff, the brilliant nerd, had finally got it right and created a time travel program that I used in the first chapter to see my mom, dad, Ella and my children and throughout this autobiography.

To our amazement over the next few hours we watched Nero burning Rome, Caesar stabbed at the Forum, Hannibal crossing the Alps with his elephants, Socrates debating Glaucon, Washington crossing the Delaware and Antony and Cleopatra making love (she was not very pretty but very sexy). We congratulated Allan for his great achievement and decided to call it OMNI for omniscient or all-knowing. His program was published in the *Oxford Science Journal* later that month and overnight nerdy Allan became the most famous scientist on the planet. He later created a simple program of OMNI that could run on a laptop.

We had a lot of fun over the next few days watching history in the hologram and solving some of its mysteries. We discovered that Jack the Ripper, who had killed and mutilated at least five women in London in 1888 was indeed the suspected Lizzie Williams (she did it because she had been jilted by so many men for other pretty women), that Nikita Khrushchev, Premier of the ancient Soviet Union, had engineered the assassination of American President John F. Kennedy on November 22, 1963 in Dallas, Texas in revenge for the embarrassing blockade of Cuba (the KGB had trained Lee Harvey Oswald and then arranged for Jack Ruby to kill him because he was dying of cancer and could not live to be examined), that American Teamster union leader Jimmy Hoffa was killed on July 30, 1975 in a suburb of Detroit by a Mafia by contract killer Richard Kuklinski and his body was crushed in a small Japanese car and sent overseas and that Plato's mysterious Atlantis that supposedly vanished beneath the waves centuries ago was the Greek Island of Santorini in the Aegean Sea which had erupted during his time which he believed destroyed it. Allan was giddy, Mary was impressed and I was fascinated but concerned about the consequences of Allan's discovery.

Eventually some unforeseen consequences developed due to Allan's program. The first was the eerie awareness that people in the future are watching us today, which robbed humans of their privacy— everyone in the future knew what you were doing now. The second was the ascendency of justice and astonishing drop in crime. With OMNI, the authorities immediately knew who had committed a crime, who was lying and what their intention had been. People could no longer act with impunity and the word criminal gradually began to fade from human vocabulary. A result of all this was a gradual modification of human behavior because people could no longer wear a mask—it was more difficult to think one way and act another without being discovered. OMNI also took all the guesswork out of history. It was no longer interpreted but rather watched.

A few weeks later I was thrilled to use OMNI to solve a longstanding problem in philosophy. At another faculty meeting tempers had not cooled much and a heated debate arose over the obscure question whether Hume had intended reason *is* or *ought* the slave of the passions. Tempers flared so I yelled stop and follow me! Surprised the faculty followed me to Allan's Laboratory and into his hologram. Allan dialed us back to David Hume in his musty book-filled study in Edinburgh, Scotland in 1739 when he was 23 writing his *Treatise of Human Nature*. It was dim due to the oil lamps but we could see him mumbling, writing, crossing out and rewriting. Rapt we finally watched him say Ah-ha and wrote *ought*. Everyone went quiet because they now knew he thought passion rules and the issue disappeared. This meant a lot to me at that time because *ought* was what my experience was telling me is true.

At the end of my time at Oxford I ominously learned that the Killing Zone Heat that had stalled for years at 40 degrees longitude in central north California had recently started advancing north again. During its stall, earth had warmed an average 24 percent, in 2000 its average temperature had been 58 degrees Fahrenheit and it was now about 72 degrees—or 14 degrees warmer. The effects had been devastating. Crops had died up, forests had disappeared, the seas had risen, flooding coastal towns, the seas had lost most of their upper levels of oxygen, killing 50% of sea animals, the glaciers of Greenland and Antarctica had melted and the equatorial regions had become uninhabitable deserts. Because of this there had been mass migrations northward (and southward in the southern hemisphere) escaping the heat causing crowding, disease, conflict and famine in the few remaining places humans could exist.

The biosphere is a narrow 12-mile band around the earth within which humans can only exist in a five-mile band above the planet surface. The altitude, for example, above 26,246 feet or 4.9 miles on Mt. Everest, is when the Death Zone begins. Above the biosphere is space at -454 degrees Fahrenheit and no oxygen and below it the center of the earth is 10,800 degrees Fahrenheit, which also has no oxygen. Humans die quickly in both places. This five-mile band is the only place in the universe humans can survive. I thought how tragic it is that humankind had unwittingly destroyed their only tiny place of existence. Because of global warming there had been a frenzy of effort early in the century to colonize space, but it was quickly discovered without earth's biosphere base life elsewhere could not be sustained. Global warming had become the worst disaster to befall humankind.

Many things came to a head in 2220 that caused the urge to move on. The first was that Mary, who had aged much faster than me, had come down with dementia. I took care of her as long as I could but eventually had to move her into a nursing home where she died in 2219 at age 90. I was devastated at losing my old-age companion. The second was that I was finally beginning to feel the effects of aging at 60. My joints hurt, I ached all over, I was weaker, forgetful and it took forever to pee. Because I hurt, I just did not care about much anymore.

The third reason was more profound—I had decided reason cannot solve human problems or bring happiness. Like my other life pursuits of pleasure, wealth, prestige, power, learning and spirituality reason turned out to be fruitless. I had watched rational philosophers get mindlessly angry and fistfight like adolescent teenagers and observed how human reason could not address threatening global warming. I decided Hume was right; reason is the servant of the stubborn passions, which makes it impotent. The last reason was more practical: it had been getting uncomfortably hot at Oxford.

So, I gave my notice to the Vice Chancellor, tried to call Albert at RC Holdings but learned they had gone out of business because all holdings had been occupied or burned, I converted the last twenty thousand of my $5 million to gold, the only remaining currency of value, said goodbye to Allan and some colleagues, packed my bags and, like I had 247 years earlier, hitchhiked out of Oxford to the airport. From there I took one of the last Icelandic Airlines flights to the Yukon.

CHAPTER 11

Resignation and the End of Life

61
(2221-2250)

I landed in Dawson, Yukon late in the evening. I had chosen the Northwest Territories just north of the Yukon to homestead because it was rapidly becoming one of the few remaining habitable places on earth. It had been an arctic zone and was now a temperate zone and as I would later learn soon to be a semi-tropical zone. About the only area on earth similar to it was the ancient region of Patagonia in the southern hemisphere.

I expected to find some place north of Dawson, buy a small cabin and live out the rest of my life in sedentary peace and solitude. To my surprise what I got was one of the greatest ordeal adventures of my life. In Dawson it seemed like I had entered a time-warp of the mid-1800s American Wild West. There were open saloons everywhere, people were rowdy and drunk, there was fighting in the streets and everyone had a gun. One drunken sot took offense at my out-of-place Oxford tweed jacket and said he wanted to fight me! I said thanks, perhaps another time and quickly moved on. Dawson turned out to be a lawless place filled with desperate and dangerous people who did not believe in a tomorrow. This was no Oxford place of polite fisticuffs but rather a fight to live or die primitive culture that became perhaps the most dangerous time of my life. I quickly had to learn the ways of Rome.

I checked into the Dawson City Hotel and got up early in the morning and went straight to an Outfitters store where I bought provisions, then to a gunsmith and bought two revolvers and a holster, which I always wore loaded, and a bullet swaging machine. I needed a rifle and while looking around to my surprise found a dusty old M4 Carbine Commando grenade launcher just like the one I had owned, which I also bought along with grenades. I then went to a clothier and got rugged leather clothes, cowboy boots, a western hat and a long rain-resistant overcoat. Finally, I went to the stables and bought two very strong horses and gear. I needed all this because I had decided to go to Aklavik in Northwest Territories on the Mackenzie River about 300 miles north of Dawson to settle. It was as far north one can go beyond the Arctic Circle at 70 degrees longitude before hitting the Beaufort Sea and would be the last place affected by the advancing heat.

While in the stable, a middle-aged strangely familiar looking Chinese man approached me and asked if I was Hugh Dangerton past president of the UNH. Guarded I said maybe, he smiled and said his name was Jim Barrow a trapper and was there getting horses for a trip north with five other trappers and I was welcome to join them. I said sure, met his companions Chris Anderson, James Irving along with Bill, Irvin and Alex, none of whom knew who I was, and we headed off north into the wilderness.

It got eerily quiet which gave me an ominous feeling of danger as the seven of us slowly rode our way north. I noticed that there were fewer animals and imagined rustlings in the brush-I felt like we were being watched. I noticed that Jim Barrow was intensely alert and constantly surveying our surroundings. Suddenly Jim said in an authoritative tone, gentlemen we are in great danger, bunch up as close as possible, unholster your guns and be prepared to fight for your lives! No sooner had he finished when a pack of about 20 vicious, carnivorous, pack-hunting 150-pound Timber Gray Wolves burst out from the underbrush, quickly ripped to pieces a pack horse and swarmed over us. One got a hold of my horse's rear leg and another had a hold of my foot. The seven of us opened fire with everything we had—our guns were blazing, I sprayed them with rapid fire and sent a couple of exploding grenades into their mist shredding many of them. Stunned, they abruptly ran off. It had been bloody; some men and animals were badly lacerated and wolf body parts were everywhere. It was a grand fight.

We were shaking and dazed from the attack but slowly gathered our wits and continued on in close formation, fully armed, alert and ready for anything. Jim told us that the wolf population had increased tenfold because, like humans, they were being squeezed north by the heat. He said they had killed most of the animals in the territory including many unprepared people. I thought how strange it is to have been an Oxford professor just last week and now a cowboy on a horse in the wilderness fighting wolves for my life! I also learned a little more about Jim Barrow. He was quiet, knowledgeable, knew the territory, its dangers and how to survive. He quickly became our acknowledged leader as we continued our journey north.

We were attacked a couple of more times, lost a few horses but fought the wolves off with preparation and firepower. After about 10 days of hard nerve-racking riding we arrived in the Northwest Territories near Aklavik and camped in a beautiful isolated grove on the Mackenzie River. After establishing a campsite and temporary barrier to keep the wolves at bay some started saying that it is too dangerous to trap so they were going back to Dawson. I said if you do you will die. We only survived because there were seven of us working together and besides that why fear them—we're humans with brains and can figure ways to defeat them—there is a reason we got to the top of the food chain. All agreed except Bill, Irvin and Alex, who left the next morning. A few months later we found their remains only a few miles from our campsite.

We immediately got to work creating a safe base homestead that was to become one of the most gratifying times of my life. Always with an armed lookout we first built a 100' X 100' enclosed stockade with timber, under the direction of Jim a large log cabin with sleeping bunks, kitchen, a grand rock fireplace and large veranda, planted a garden with potatoes and maize and acquired some cows, sheep and pigs. We were always threatened by wolves but over time shot, poisoned and trapped them into submission. As their threat subsided Jim, Chris and James trapped bountiful furs and got rich. I was surprised how quickly the soft living at Oxford turned me into a tough, strong and robust frontiersman. It felt really good to fight for life, build a homestead with my own hands and survive.

Throughout this time Jim Barrow had been an enigma—there had always been something about him strangely familiar. When we first met he had known who I was, he had been the hero who saved us from the wolves and he had taught me how to survive a primitive life, so one day when we were alone I asked him outright who he was. He smiled and said I am Bodhi's son, that he had left Lhasa because of the heat after his dad died, had traveled across northern China and spent many years in Alaska and the Yukon as trapper. He said he had changed last name to Borrow because it was Western and that his dad had talked a lot about me. I was incredulously stunned, hugged him and said I loved his dad. With that Jim Barrow became the last great friend of my life.

After a few years on the homestead I had spent all of my $20,000 in gold for provisions, building materials, animals and crops and for the first time in my life was truly penniless. This did not bother me so much because living a primitive life required little money. It felt good to live simply. However, providence smiled on me one day when I was exploring some territory downriver. I stumbled across this obviously manmade 20-foot-deep pit with valleys forking off on all sides and pondered what it could be. Out of curiosity I walked up one of the small valleys and started chipping away at its end when a small shiny gold rock tumbled to the ground. I realized it was a long-abandoned gold mine so I started digging more and found a rich vein of solid gold. The miners had stopped only a few feet from wealth. I was giddy with excitement, collected a pouch full of gold rocks and covered it up. My few days of poverty quickly came to an end because from then on whenever I needed money I just went to the pit and dug up some gold.

During my years on the homestead I often reminisced about my long strange life and often went back to visit it with OMNI. I would swell with emotion, watching my long-dead parents again and felt excitement seeing me in my energetic youth hitchhiking from Oxford to Southampton reciting Robert Frost's poem to take the road less traveled. It made me feel good to know that I had. I visited the places from the NYT article, my pleasure time in San Francisco, my time of wealth in New York, my becoming famous in Los Angeles, the dangerous time as president of the United Nations of Humankind, my engaging time as a writer and professor at Whitman and Oxford, my time in Lhasa and conversations with the Dali Lama and my experience getting to the homestead.

I particularly reminisced about the people I had known. It was a life-history kaleidoscope, seeing the engaging men and women like my childhood friends Jamie and Jay, Betsy, Corey, Madeline, Garrett, Noi, Bill Weatherspoon, Trish, Bill Engleson, Stella, Bodhi, Rachel, Mary Magdalene, Allan Freedenhoff as well as my old dog Thad. But above all I watched my family. I could never get enough of reliving my times with my beloved Ella and our six children John, Sybil (who I painfully watched die so young), Maude, Pete, Ella and Edward.

During the last few years I spent many hours on the veranda overlooking the Mackenzie River talking with young Jim who had become my close friend. We talked a lot about his dad Bodhi, Buddhism and Lhasa. Jim revered his dad and, knowing my history, had great respect for my knowledge—he asked my many questions about life. One time he asked me what were my most important life lessons. I thought for a long time and then said I learned many things but I think there are three. The first is to love and be loved. I said I spent many wasted years pursuing desires for excitement, pleasure, wealth, prestige, power and later for knowledge, spirituality and reason but they were all transient. Every time I achieved them the desire disappeared. I said John Stuart Mill had asked if it is better to be a pig satisfied or Socrates dissatisfied and I think neither—both are always just more of the same. Then I said love is different. I had loved many people and it is the only thing that endured. For me, love satisfied a simple basic instinct and fulfilled me. Nnature is easily satisfied.

The second is to live within nature because it always bats last. I said it seems every time humans disrupt nature's natural patterns, problems arise. There was a movement once long ago to make humans unisex that resulted in a hermaphroditic unisex person that produced impotent enervated offspring. I said it is best to reproduce within nature's chance rather than human design, which puzzled Jim. I then described how global warming, nuclear weapons and overpopulation were further examples of human interference with nature that might extinguish our species. Jim was not puzzled but rather horrified with this lesson.

Finally, I said the most significant lesson I learned is the importance of my time. This one caught Jim's interest and he asked why. I said our time is like an original masterpiece painting and everything else is just a copy. Our parents, the people we grew up with, our first love, our wife and the children we procreate are all originals that cannot be reproduced—they are irreplaceable. I paused and then in a low emotional voice said being married to Ella and creating a family of six children was the deepest, most natural and meaningful experience of my long life. I think it touched the very essence of happiness. I paused again and then said people are so caught up in their daily work and cares they never see the big picture and never appreciate what they have. I know this because I lived beyond my time and tried to recapture its essence in various ways, but it was always beyond my grasp. I have discovered that living forever is empty and pointless. It was interesting but always just more of the same. After another long pause I said Jim, I long for my time and the people in it I loved. I wish I had died with Ella.

I spent the last year of my life a wizened old man in the Northwest Territories on my homestead veranda writing this autobiography. We had taken down the stockade walls long ago when the wolves left so I had a grand view of the wide Mackenzie River. I lived simply and peacefully, weary and tired from my long life, slowly withdrawing from existence while waiting for the inevitable. I often thought of my ancient family from another age and longed to join them.

Many years ago at Whitman I had read an autobiographical lament by Frederick Locker Lampson, a nineteenth-century Englishman poet and man of letters, in his *Confidences*. It so expressed my view of life I reproduce it here with a few modifications.

> I am so far resigned to my lot that I feel small pain at the thought of having to part from what has been called the pleasant habit of existence, the sweet fable of life. I would not care to live my wasted life over again, and so to prolong my artificially extended span. I humbly submit because it is a Law of Nature, and my appointed destiny. I dread the increase of infirmities, so let me slip away as quietly and comfortably as I can. Let the end come, if peace come with it. I do not know that there is a great deal to be said for this world, or our sojourn here upon it; but it has pleased Nature so to place us, and it must please me also. I ask you, what is human life? Is not it maimed happiness—care and weariness, weariness and care, with the baseless expectation, the strange cozenage of a brighter tomorrow? At best it is but a forward child that must be played with and humored, to keep it quiet till it falls asleep, and at worst a rebellious teenager who must be endured til' they fly the nest. I gratefully part this existence to rest in eternal peace.

In 2250 when I was 61 it had got so hot I had to stay under cover during the day, could not sleep at night because it never cooled off, and all the trees and vegetation were rapidly dying and turning brown at the homestead. The Killing Zone Heat had started advancing again 30 years ago in 2220 and made all of the Pacific Northwest, including my hometown of Portland and most of Canada, uninhabitable. I had been told that most of the center part of the globe had burned and now looked much like the parched planet Mercury. I knew the end was near, so I stopped writing this autobiography because I thought it was pointless to be writing for a nonexistent future reader. Whoever you are reading this, you must have found it on my laptop hard drive where I left it.

It was in the early very hot fall when I got this inexplicable urge to see the gravesite and monument I had prepared for myself on the homestead overlooking the river. While I was inspecting my final resting place I tripped, knocked over my tombstone, fell horribly, hobbled home and lay on the veranda in terrible pain. I decided that this was my day to die, September 25, 2250, exactly 300 years from my birth. The inscription on my tombstone was:

Reggie Calhoun
(aka Hugh Dangerton)
1950-2250
I Knew This Would Happen

www.ingramcontent.com/pod-product-compliance
Lightning Source LLC
Chambersburg PA
CBHW070631120726
47909CB00004B/1386